CW00433751

Author's Note

This story is a cozy murder mystery and as such is a work of fiction. Any similarity to actual persons, events, or places is purely coincidental with the exception of the island of Crete, which really is that beautiful. However, it is not a travel guide to today's Crete. The Crete of 1919 would have been very different from the Crete of today. Many of today's roads had yet to be built, so the route our adventurers travel would be very different nowadays, and often much quicker! Also, for the purposes of storytelling the positioning of some of the places described are not quite the same as you will find on a map. Most notably, if you ever get a chance to see Knossos (and please do, it's wonderful!) then, unlike our travellers, you will probably go on the coast road to Heraklion first, then inland up into the hills to Knossos second. Having said all that, if you do visit Crete, you will see many beautiful sights and locations along the way. Maybe you will remember something from this story and in your mind's eye you will see how beautiful and wonderful Crete would have looked a hundred years ago!

Chapter 1

Alex woke up in the narrow bunk, covered in a heavy, cold sweat. He was freezing. His covers lay kicked off on the floor. He lay there for several minutes, unable to move. He was fighting to get back control. His head was still filled with the images from his nightmare. His heart was racing. Over the last three years he'd had the same nightmare multiple times. Each nightmare always seemed to follow a similar path, forcing him to relive the experiences that had happened three years ago.

Almost always it began with him on the deck of the battlecruiser. Shells would start hitting the ship. The sound of the explosions would be deafening. Fires would erupt all around him. He would try to find his way through them, but by some surreal logic, as he moved towards a gap in the ring of fire, it would disappear and reappear somewhere else. The flames would grow closer. He would look down and see the fire hose in his hand. Sometimes he could persuade it to give an ineffectual dribble of water. Sometimes nothing. Sometimes he would look around and see that the hose ended in a ragged torn off mess a few feet behind him. Throughout he would feel the terror rising inside him. The worst thing was that he would know with certainty what would come next. He would look up and see the wreck of the superstructure above him begin to topple. In slow motion, with the searchlight mounted on it still blazing into the night, it would describe a graceful arc, falling towards him. Often it was here that he would awake. Usually because his own screams, muffled by his still closed lips, would wake him up.

If his muffled screams did wake him, he was lucky. But as often as not the nightmare would keep on forcing him to relive the most terrifying part of his experience. He would be pinned under the wreckage. He would struggle to drag himself out. At least in the nightmare, his leg was numb, unlike the searing pain he had felt in real life. But the leg would still pin him in place. He would twist and turn, but he wouldn't be able to free himself. All the time, all around him, the fires would be closing in. Sometimes he would imagine the flames had reached him and his uniform was on fire. He would try to beat the flames out with his hands. Sometimes he would dream that he had managed the impossible and lifted the wreckage off himself, but he would still be unable to move. It was as if his injured leg was glued to the deck.

Alex still lay there on his sweat soaked mattress. Because he had lived through the nightmare again and again, reliving those same terrifying memories, it now seemed to him that the nightmare was like a tangible creature living in the back of his brain. During the day, hidden and invisible, but still there. Always waiting to come out of hiding and attack him at night. He never knew what seemingly random daytime experience would trigger the creature. He lay there struggling to make his brain stop going over and over the same terrifying visions. He had to fight off the overpoweringly strong grip the images had on his brain. Some things were on his side though. He'd suffered the nightmare many times, but that meant he'd learnt how to fight back against the after effects of the nightmare.

Distraction was a key tool. Any distraction. Doing maths in his head sometimes worked. Counting something, anything that was around him, sometimes worked. But tonight, he was struggling. Stubbornly he fought to push the effects of the nightmare away.

He suddenly realised that his eyes were looking at the full moon. A turn of the ships course must have swung it into view through his porthole. The moon hung there, huge and bright and impossible to ignore. He hung on to it, a drowning man finding a piece of floating wreckage. As his breathing came under control, his heart slowed. After several minutes he swung his legs out of the high sided bunk. He nearly stumbled and fell forward onto the floor, as his weak left leg failed to take his weight. Supporting himself with his hands on the bunk's edge, he worked his way over to the small chest of drawers and the well stuffed horsehair chair on the far side of his cabin. Rifling through his suit jacket, thrown over the back of the chair, he was disgusted to find his pockets empty of cigarettes.

Resignedly, he dragged his clothes on and grabbing his walking stick, left his cabin.

Chapter 2

Alex slowly climbed the stairs to the promenade on the top deck and, upon reaching it, for a few minutes he breathed in the clean fresh air coming off the Mediterranean Sea, before entering the first-class salon. It was papered in a plush red velvet wallpaper, with red shaded wall lights. The ceiling was dark wood panelling with exposed wooden beams. Gilt framed paintings of hunting and fishing scenes decorated the walls. Not surprisingly at nearly one o'clock in the morning, it was nearly deserted. The only ones there were the young steward behind the bar and a rather dignified elderly gentleman, seated at one of the groups of four brown leather barrel chairs.

Trying not to make eye contact with the elderly gentleman, Alex limped across the lounge to the bar steward.

Catching his attention Alex said, "Excuse me. Large scotch, no water please. Oh, and do you sell any English brands of cigarettes?"

The steward quickly poured the scotch and passed it to Alex. Looking below the bar he said, "I'm very sorry sir. No cigarettes left at all. I think we ran out just after we left Corfu." Alex sagged. He took a large sip of his scotch and leant forward heavily on the bar.

Behind him, a soft English voice said, "Excuse me, but I have a nearly full packet, if you'd like one? They're only Capstans I'm afraid, but I'd be happy to share them . . . "

Alex turned and saw the elderly gentleman smiling at him. He had risen from his table where he had been reading a book and come up to the bar. He looked to be about sixty years old. He was slightly built, grey haired and on his way to going bald, but with long white sideburns and a thick moustache. He was wearing a light linen suit.

Alex's desire for nicotine fought with his reluctance to have a conversation, but the desire for nicotine was stronger.

Leaning on his walking stick in his left hand he reached out with his right for one of the proffered cigarettes.

Without meeting the stranger's eyes, he mumbled "Er. . . Thanks. Much appreciated." As his fingers teased a cigarette from the pack, they trembled and the cigarette fell from them onto the bar.

"My fault," said the elder man quickly and picked up and offered the cigarette a second time. "My name's Thomas Crompton. How do you do?"

"Er . . .Very well, thank you." Alex realised reluctantly that he would have to introduce himself, "Alex Armstrong".

The old man smiled "Enjoying the voyage? Or maybe not such a good sailor?"

"Yes . . . er . . no. I mean the voyage is OK. I'm ex-navy, so I'm fine"

"If you don't mind me saying, you don't look fine. You look a little shaky. Why don't you sit down and finish your drink here, in comfort?"

Alex hesitated. He really wanted to just sit by himself and finish his cigarette and drink, but years of ingrained politeness and respect for his elders forced him to reluctantly accept the offer. They moved away from the bar, to the table where the gentleman had left his book. He took the seat furthest from the elderly gentleman. For the first time, he actually made eye-to-eye contact with him and saw that he was being quietly studied.

"I'm ex-navy too – Surgeon-Commodore actually, but I don't like to use the rank now."

Looking for a safe conversational topic, Alex asked "I joined the ship in Brindisi. You too?"

The old man paused before replying. Without looking up, Alex got the feeling he was still being studied by the old man.

"Yes, I lived there before the war and then retired there after the war."

The last thing Alex wanted to do was talk about the war with another old sailor, so he tried to move the conversation on. "I'm leaving the ship in Crete – My uncle and cousin have a business there, in Port Chania."

The old man paused and continued to study Alex. He saw a pleasant, boyish looking young man with unruly light brown hair, maybe just a little over six foot tall. He looked about twenty-five years old, clean shaven with intelligent but worried eyes. Eventually he replied, "Same for me old chap. Except after leaving the boat in Chania, I'm travelling by land to Knossos. I'll use the land transport provided by a subsidiary of the shipping line to get me to Knossos." He paused again to take a sip of his drink. "Interesting place Knossos, you know. King Minos. The Minotaur. Lot of myths, good stories and that sort of stuff."

Alex took another sip of his drink. Feeling a little calmer he said, "Well if you have trouble with getting the transport, look me up. I'm sure my uncle or cousin have contacts."

"Thanks old man – I may take you up on that." He looked across at Alex's glass. "Would you like another drink?"

Alex also looked at his glass and was surprised to see how quickly it had gone down. "Thanks, but no thanks," he said. He picked it up and drained the last dregs. "I think I'll take the cigarette you so kindly gave me, smoke it on the promenade deck, then try to get some sleep."

Alex smiled again at the older man and, pushing with his undamaged leg, slowly managed to slide his chair back to clear the table. Carefully positioning his stick, he used it to lever himself up. Smiling once more at the old man and nodding a thanks to the steward, he limped out of the salon.

Lord Thomas, Surgeon-Commodore retired, watched him go. He had worked on thousands of injured soldiers behind the trenches in France. He was grateful that his medical skills, together with modern medicine, had made it possible for him to save so many of those lives – but too many had not survived. Sadly, he'd also seen many with injuries not just to the body, but to their minds as well. Despite his best efforts, none of his medical skills or medicines had worked in treating that type of injury. Watching Alex limp from the salon, he had the feeling that he had just met one more of those casualties of war.

Chapter 3

The next morning, Alex left his cabin on deck four and slowly climbed the stairs to the promenade deck and walked along to the first-class breakfast room for an early breakfast, He had slept fitfully until about 6:00am, when he'd decided that further sleep was impossible. He washed and dressed slowly and carefully, then decided to go and see what was available for breakfast, even though it was well before the time that breakfast was officially scheduled to be served. However, in the breakfast room one long table was already set for breakfast. Only one seat was occupied, by a short, slightly portly, middle-aged man, dressed in expensive black dinner jacket, black trousers and a low-cut waistcoat. Alex took note of the heavy gold watch and chain in the waistcoat and the conspicuously large gold cuff-links that the stranger was wearing. The stranger smiled at Alex and greeted him with a cheerful greeting of, "Bore Da!"

Alex smiled back and returned his own, "Bore Da" greeting.

"Oh. So it's you that's a Welshman as well, is it?" asked the stranger.

"No" replied Alex with a smile, but I've come across a few in my time and I know that 'Bora Da' means 'Good Morning' in Welsh"

"Well sit you down and be comfy. I bet you weren't expecting to find a Welshman on this fine little boat, sailing over this lovely Mediterranean Sea, now were you?

"I must admit I'm a little surprised" replied Alex "And also to find one that is quite this cheerful at this time in the morning.

"Well for a hard-working Welshman, this is no time at all. My name is Dafydd Williams – Dai if you like – but I'd prefer not Taff or Taffy. Please to meet you, it is."

"I would never dream of calling you Taff, Dai. And I'd be very happy if you'd call me Alex."

At this point the white jacketed waiter approached with a plate and placed it down in front of Dai. Alex glanced at the plate and saw smoked herring, sausages, grilled ham, fried eggs and potato slices.

"Well, that looks like a breakfast suitable for a hard-working Welshman if ever I saw one," said Alex.

"Well I asked for laverbread as well, but the poor lad seemed to think I wanted something from a volcano, so I think it's going to be a long time 'till I taste that bread of heaven again, isn't it."

Alex nodded to the waiter. He ordered coffee and his own, much more modest breakfast. "I was surprised to see anyone up this early in the morning, Dai. And more surprised to see breakfast being served. So, what caused you to shake a leg this early in the morning?"

"The table is set and breakfast served for the officers, but the staff seem happy to serve anyone. As for me being up and about at this hour, the truth it is that this is more a late night for me than an early morning. I got in with a terrible bad crowd of card players last night and we played poker 'till the early hours, didn't we. Terrible bad lot of men, they were. Not at all the sort you would find in our chapel back home in the valleys."

"And did you make a profit Dai?" Alex asked with a smile.

"Well, I won a little and lost a little." said Dai, with a dead pan look on his face. Alex could get no feel from his expression whether Dai had been successful or not. Alex decided that Dai probably had the ideal poker face and could have lost a year's salary last night and still show no trace of it in his expression.

"So, you enjoy a little gamble Dai?"

"Not a regular thing for me, at all. What I enjoy most is buying cheap and selling high. It's worked very well for me in the past and I'm hoping it will continue to work well for me in the future."

"So, what sort of thing do you buy and sell?" asked Alex.

Oh, a little of this and a little of that. Whatever I can get my hands on that's in high demand and I can get a decent price for." Dai's face had quickly reverted to that blank expression again. Alex thought of the black-marketeers during the war that would also have adopted that same phrase as their motto. ". . . and what about you, Alex bach? Are you in the buying and selling lark too?"

"No." Alex replied. "I have some business with my uncle and cousin in Crete and I will stay there for a couple of weeks. I'm also hoping for a little vacation in the warmth."

"Well, I'm off to even warmer climes than you are then, I am. I'll be on the next boat from Heraklion to Cairo, where I'm told the heat will be plenty warm enough for this hard-working Welshman from the beautiful valleys and mountains of Wales!"

"Well best of luck Dai. If there is anything I can help with when we get to Chania, let me know. If not, I'll be sure to say goodbye before we go our different ways."

"That's a very kind offer, Alex bach. I'd appreciate that. But right now, I'll leave you to your fine breakfast and make my way back to my little bed to enjoy some well-deserved sleep." With that Dai Williams rose and wished Alex a good day. After Dai had left, Alex looked in surprise at Dai's plate, which he had managed to clear even while also holding up his end of the conversation! A healthy appetite was obviously one of the characteristics of a hard-working Welshman!

After finishing his breakfast, Alex returned to his cabin. For a while he half considered remaining in his cabin all day. He had the excuse of catching up on his lost sleep. However, in the end he decided that it felt too much like hiding for him to be comfortable with that as a course of action. In the end he compromised. For the rest of the morning, he rested in his bunk and dozed, off and on. He eventually finished the book he had brought with him around midday. Calling for the steward, he asked for a lunch tray to be brought to his cabin. When the steward arrived with the tray, he also brought an unexpected note, inviting him to dinner at the captain's table. He hated eating in public, or at any event where he felt he became the centre of attention. He always felt that pitying eyes were watching him as he limped along. When recuperating in England, he'd been invited to dinner at several different manor houses. The tradition of parading into dinner arm-in-arm, accompanied by whichever eligible young lady the hosts thought appropriate, had been agony for him. After the second such event, he'd started to find reasons to refuse any further invitations. He was much happier dining by himself. This evening, he had half a thought to again have dinner served in his cabin. Unfortunately, his ingrained sense of respect towards a ship's captain and his innate sense of what was proper behaviour, made it impossible for him to decline the invite. He reluctantly informed the steward that he would attend.

Murder on Crete

By the time he had finished his excellent lunch, accompanied by a glass of refreshing white wine, he had put thoughts of this evening behind him and he was beginning to feel more uplifted and even invigorated. He left his cabin and made his way up to the promenade deck, where he looked for a deckchair in an isolated position so he could enjoy the sun without being disturbed. He settled back with the sun warming his face and considered his future.

His term of service in the navy had come to an end, earlier than most, since those who had been wounded were demobilised, or 'demobbed' first. The Admiralty was in the process of closing the office he was currently assigned to in Brindisi. They had made him an offer for him to re-enlist and move him back to an office in London, there to join a newly formed department. After more than a year of working practically round the clock without taking any leave, he'd asked for and been granted some leave, to rest, recuperate and to consider the offer. After a few weeks with his uncle and cousin in Crete, he expected he would be returning to England one way or another – either to take up the post the Admiralty had offered him, or to stay with his older brother in his small manor house on the Isle of Wight.

If he was honest with himself, neither held much attraction for him. After his father had died, his older brother had taken over running the family manor house and farm and was making a good job of it. He knew his brother would welcome him back to the family home, but Alex really didn't see where he would fit in or how he would earn his keep. He didn't want to accept something that he worried would be very close to charity. His other choice was to stay in the navy. He felt that during the fighting, he had done important work, but after his injury he'd been mostly office bound. Now that the war-to-end-all-wars was over, would the work be as satisfying? But most of all he felt restless, wanting to be out of the office, to try something new, have new experiences, see new things. His mind wondered, with thoughts of other lives he could lead, until eventually he drifted into sleep under the warming Mediterranean sun.

Chapter 4

That evening he dressed for dinner and arrived at the first-class dining room early. When dining in public, Alex always made a point of arriving early if he could and trying to be unobtrusively seated before other guests arrived. He disliked the attention he felt he received from other guests as he made his limping entrance and struggled to seat himself. Tonight, he entered the dining room early and looked around. He was impressed with the quality and décor of the room, being more used to the spartan standards of naval ships. Wood panelling covered the lower half of the walls. Elegant chandeliers hung over the half dozen tables. Oil paintings, spotlighted with wall lights, decorated the walls. Most of the paintings showed seascapes, either of beautiful harbours or of square-rigged sailing ships battling against the sea. The tables glittered with crystal and silverware. The captain stood out as the only diner in a uniform. It was white, with double breasted jacket and dark blue epaulets, with the distinctive gold rings of a captain on its sleeves. He was a little surprised and dismayed to see three other guests had arrived before him and were seated at the captain's table, already in conversation with the captain. The seated guests consisted of an older, married couple and an elegantly dressed young man, with slicked back, black hair and a pencil thin moustache.

As he approached the group, the captain rose and introduced him to the other guests. He spoke in very good English but with a slight French accent. "Good evening, sir." Turning to those already seated, he said, "May I introduce Lieutenant Alex Armstrong." Alex was surprised that the captain already knew his name. Turning back to Alex, he offered him the seat on his left and introduced the other, already seated dinner guests. "This gentleman is Sir Alfred Jeffries and these are Mr. George and Mrs. Millicent Webster. Alex acknowledged the polite responses of Mr. and Mrs. Webster together with the merest nod that Sir Alfred gave him. After that the captain paused before sitting and held Alex's gaze for a few seconds. He appeared to be awaiting a further response from Alex, but eventually he smiled and nodded to Alex and finally seated himself. A waiter quietly and discretely appeared behind Alex and drew back the gilded dining chair on the left of the captain for Alex to be seated. Alex placed both hands on the table to support himself, as the waiter took his walking stick from him. Alex lowered himself gingerly and carefully into the chair before awkwardly shuffling forward to the table. Looking up at the waiter, Alex nodded his thanks. The waiter smiled back and leant the walking stick against the arm of his chair.

Alex saw that the captain was also still smiling at him, which set Alex back, thinking that his difficulty had amused the captain in some way.

"I think that perhaps your memory is not so good," said the captain, with an even broader smile.

"Not at all," said Alex "My memory is perfectly fine."

"Well perhaps," said the captain, "but you should maybe remember me?"

Alex studied the captain's features, but his blank expression gave away the fact the he still did not recognise the captain.

"Perhaps if you are imagining me a little less elegantly dressed than you see me now? Dirty, soaked to the skin, climbing from your ships boat onto the deck of your ship? In the Dardanelles in 1915?

Alex's eyes widened. He studied the captain more closely. ". . . . the Lieutenant from the French battleship Bouvet . . ?"

The captain's face split into a still wider grin. "Yes, mon ami! Francois Meunier, Lieutenant as I was then! My ship was struck by a mine and sank that day. I was one of the lucky ones to be picked up by a boat sent from your ship."

Now Alex began to smile too. "Oh yes, I remember you now. You climbed over the ships rail, face black with smoke from the fires on your ship, half your uniform ripped away. You came to attention and gave me the smartest salute, then asked for permission to come aboard! I remember thinking what a crazy Frenchman!"

"I was told one must always respect British etiquette," said the captain, shrugging.

Alex turned to the other guests and explained, "and the next day, when my ship, the HMS Southampton, went back into battle, Francois 'volunteered' his few uninjured matelots together with himself to form a damage control party."

"Oui and let me tell you, the next day was 'a hot one' as you English say. We had much work to do."

"Yes," agreed Alex. "After the battle, we were forced to withdraw to Lemnos. I thought the Southampton might have to be scrapped, she was so badly damaged, but she was dry docked and eventually repaired."

"To the battleship Bouvet and HMS Southampton," said Captain Meunier, raising his glass. "In the British Naval traditional, I toast you while remaining seated."

Murder on Crete

Smiling Alex raised his water glass and returned the captain's toast.

As the captain returned his glass to the table, two further guests arrived. Alex was a little surprised when the gentleman who had introduced himself last night as merely Thomas Crompton, was introduced by the captain as Lord Thomas Crompton. The second man was short and slightly built, almost sparrow like, practically bald with just wisps of white hair above his ears, and the slightly bulbous nose with the dominant red blood vessels of a serious drinker. He was wearing a rather old-fashioned dinner jacket, with a high collar shirt and gold rimmed spectacles. The captain introduced him as Doctor Constantine Papadopoulos. The captain offered the dining chair on his right to Lord Thomas and Doctor Papadopoulos walked around the table to take the vacant seat between the lord and Mrs. Webster and her husband. As Lord Thomas moved around the table to take his seat, Alex looked up with a questioning expression on his face, surprised to discover his acquaintance from last night had a title. Lord Thomas noted the surprise in Alex's eyes and the eyebrows raised in query. Lord Thomas smiled, guessing what was going through the younger man's mind.

Mr. Webster rose and shook Lord Thomas's hand. "Very good to meet you, my lord. I'm afraid we're not used to being around so many titles."

"Too many ranks and titles around anyway nowadays to my liking" Lord Thomas said to the other diners. "Doesn't mean a damn thing in my opinion. In my life I've seen men with no rank or title achieve the darndest things, things that leave me in awe."

"Well, I think rank and title are still essential for an orderly way of life," said Sir Alfred, seated on the same side as Alex, separated from him by an as yet unfilled chair. "Too many blasted protesters since the war ended, demanding no-end of changes to all that is great about our country."

Alex studied Sir Alfred for a moment. He thought him to be about thirty-five years old. His swept-back hair and moustache were immaculately trimmed. His overall appearance was quite good looking, except for a downturned lip that gave him the appearance of a perpetual sneer. His fashionable dinner jacket and waistcoat were clearly very expensive. The waistcoat appeared to be fastened with jewelled studs. Alex felt a little self-conscious and underdressed in his old Royal Navy, mess undress jacket.

Lord Thomas looked up. "Seems to me change is inevitable. We're living in the age of invention. If the government don't think that will bring about change in our society, then I think they are mistaken. Better they lead from the front than dig themselves in. Thinking like that led to the war in the trenches. Inventions like the tank brought an end to that sort of thinking." Lord Thomas nodded to the waiter and accepted a glass of sherry.

"Exactly my point," replied Sir Alfred. "We've been bred to know what's good for the population and educated on how to lead them. We know what's good for them and need to make that clear." Turning to the waiter at his side he snapped "Not sherry man! That's a whisky glass in front of me and the damn things empty!"

Lord Thomas looked directly at Sir Alfred, "From what I saw of the military command in France, I'm not sure that titles are necessarily a good indication of knowing what's best for anyone."

Murder on Crete

The captain tactfully decided now might be the time to redirect the conversation, before it became more heated. "Doctor Papadopoulos, I believe you to be a good friend of Prince George of Greece?"

"Yes captain. In fact, I would have left Corfu on a much earlier ship, but for having to attend to a severe illness of Princess Eugénie, the Prince's youngest child."

"All's well with the little girl now I hope?" interjected Mrs Webster

"For certainty. The child is now very healthy and hopefully she has a long, happy future in front of her."

Alex turned to the captain and enquired, "And what about our future, captain? Are we making good time for Crete, sir?"

"Yes, mon ami. Good time. The Mediterranean can always throw up a little surprise, but the weather forecast is good and we should reach Crete in two days, on-time."

Alex nodded, then noticed the captain begin to rise from his seat. Then he saw that both Sir Alfred, Mr. Webster and Lord Thomas, had also risen.

The captain looked back over Alex's shoulders and said "Gentlemen – may I introduce Miss Karolina McAllister."

Alex twisted round to glimpse the new arrival who he realised was standing directly behind his chair. She was slim and very attractive, with blonde silky hair cut in a Dutch Bob. She had strong chin and cheek bones and a broad smile with full lips. Probably her most distinctive attributes were her wide, crystal blue eyes. She was wearing a silk evening dress in dark blue, with a dropped waist highlighted by a broad contrasting light blue sash. The square neckline drew attention to a double string of pearls. The dress was cut in the modern fashion, to end just below the knee and to make the best of her slim figure. She wore very little makeup, just a little lipstick and eyeshadow. The combined effect on Alex was stunning. Belatedly Alex realised he had been staring at her for several seconds and that all the other men at the table were on their feet as she waited to be seated between him and Sir Alfred.

He turned back to the table, intending to stand as quickly as he could. As he reached for his stick, propped at the side of his chair, he knocked it to the floor. Still trying to get to his feet quickly, he decided to ignore the stick and tried to push back his chair from the table. Unable to lift himself fully from the chair when using just his one good leg, the chair refused to budge. Giving up with that attempt, he tried again to lean over and pick up his stick from where it lay on the floor. It was just out of reach. In desperation he put both hands on the edge of the table, intending to use his arms alone to lift his weight from the chair.

At that moment, Karolina glanced at each of the men standing and said, "That's very nice of you gentlemen, but please, be seated". Turning to Alex, who she saw was still seated, she gave him a frosty glance, before seating herself in the dining chair next to him.

Sir Alfred gave Karolina a smile that only reached his mouth and not his eyes. He said, "Well my dear, that sounds like a Canadian or American accent?"

"American, actually. Texan to be specific."

"Over here looking to marry an English title I bet," smirked Sir Alfred. "Like so many handsome and wealthy American fillies look to do nowadays".

Karolina looked him square in his smiling face for a second or two. "Actually, I think English aristocrats are over-rated and overentitled. I've not yet met one that I would think of as a real man, compared to the men in Texas." Then still looking him directly in his eyes, she gave him a dazzling smile.

Everyone around the table paused to replay Karolina's response in their heads. Alex had been caught in the process of taking a sip of sherry. Her dead pan put-down caused him to cough and nearly choke on his drink. Once he had his breathing under control, Alex looked across the table to Sir Thomas to see that he was also trying hard to smother a laugh. He tried a surreptitious look to his side in order to see Karolina's face, but she saw him looking so he quickly looked back to the front. Sir Alfred was spluttering and couldn't put a coherent response together quickly enough.

Sir Thomas was still struggling to suppress his laughter. Smiling directly at Karolina he said, "And it appears to me that the ladies from Texas are at least an equal match to their menfolk, my dear."

Karolina nodded to Lord Thomas and accepted the complement. Meanwhile, Mrs. Webster stepped in to divert the conversation to safer territory. "Captain, may I be impertinent and ask what that unusual aperitif is that you are drinking?"

"Of course, madame. It is a French drink called Dubonnet. It was developed at the request of the French government, specifically to be acceptable to French soldiers. Its purpose is to disguise the bitter taste of quinine given to our troops operating in countries where malaria is prevalent." Signalling to one of the waiters for the table he indicated that Mrs. Webster should taste the fortified wine infused with herbs and spices.

As her glass was being filled, Mrs. Webster turned to her husband. "Perhaps this is something we should consider for our travels in Egypt?" Without waiting for his reply, she turned to Karolina and said, "That's a beautiful name, Miss McAllister, but surely Karolina is Italian?

Karolina smiled at her and corrected her pronunciation, "My mother insists it is pronounced 'Care - o - lee – nah' but I really don't care. Actually, it's origin is German. My mother, grandmother and my great grandmother were also called Karolina. My grandmother emigrated from Germany on a sailing ship in 1854. She was only a teenager at the time. Going by herself to America to marry a friend of her brother who she had never met."

"Fascinating my dear," said Lord Thomas. "I met a great number of brave Americans in the trenches towards the end of the war and found them to be both very direct and excellent company."

"You fought with the Americans sir?"

"Not fought, no. I was indeed posted to France but just to serve as a doctor. I treated many American soldiers, both for wounds and the flu. I recall being surprised that, for some reason, it appeared to me that the stronger and healthier American soldiers were even more susceptible to the influenza than the British lads that had suffered from poor rations and conditions for years."

Karolina looked shaken for a second. "My own experience would support that. My fiancé was one of the strongest, healthiest men I knew, but he too died of influenza shortly after arriving in France".

Mrs. Webster reached a hand across the table towards Kristina sympathetically. "It seems so unfair that after so many lives were lost fighting in the trenches, that nature then sought out even those who survived and ended many of their lives. Did you also come across many Americans Mr Armstrong?"

"No, Mrs. Webster," Alex smiled. "Miss Karolina is the first American I've met, although I've also heard of the bravery of the Americans. When the American soldiers arrived in France, I was sailing a desk in the Admiralty Offices in London"

Without looking at Alex, Karolina said "Some people had a luckier war than others."

Lord Thomas looked across the table at Karolina, who still looked a little pale and Alex, who now blushed bright red and wondered at how quickly the tension between them had arisen.

Again, Mrs. Webster was also quick to sense the tension and sort a way to ease it. "Are you doing a grand tour of Europe then, Miss McAllister? And please, you should call me Millicent,"

"Yes, Millicent," smiled Karolina "and please call me Karolina. Maybe not a Grand Tour in the old, traditional sense, but so far, I've seen Paris, London, Rome and Athens."

"I'm sure the social scene in London gave you many chances to indulge yourself in parties and such Miss McAllister." said Sir Alfred, a little frostily and perhaps thinking to even the score for being put in his place earlier.

"Actually, no. I was staying with a friend of my mother's, a Mrs. Edith Stoney and one of the highlights for me was to attend her lecture on the Physics and Mathematics of Steam Turbine Engines, at King's College for Women. I'm afraid her mathematics was too advanced for me, but it was enthralling to learn about the physics of the steam turbine. I also spent a considerable time in the British Museum, which I also found to be extremely good. My mother encouraged my early passion in all areas of science and knowledge and particularly history and archaeology. I've pursued both ever since."

At the mention of steam turbines, Alex had again turned to glance at her, but looked away quickly again when she noticed him looking. Lord Thomas also showed signs of interest.

"I believe I know of Edith, and also her sister Florence. I think they set up and operated the new radio-graphical services in several field hospitals during the war. When working on the wounded, I benefited greatly from what we came to call 'x-ray pictographs'. Particularly helpful when attempting to find and remove shrapnel fragments. Your mother's friend and her sister did a tremendous amount of groundbreaking work and saved many lives while doing it."

"You are absolutely correct about Edith, Lord Thomas. In fact, Edith is quite modest about it, but I did see her French Croix de Guerre medal while I was staying with her."

"Karolina, if you're happy with me calling you that, then I think you can also drop the 'Lord' when addressing me."

Karolina responded to him with a dazzling smile. "Thank you Tommy – I'll do that. I may even revise my opinion of English aristocrats . . . given time!"

Lord Thomas roared with laughter!

Alex also smiled. Hoping to redeem himself a little, he said "I also studied mathematics, at Oxford."

"Really," said Millicent, perhaps hoping to help him make a better impression, "I believe that's an extremely tough discipline, isn't it? Did you receive a bachelors, or maybe a masters?"

"Er . . . . no actually. I didn't actually graduate. . . . The war you know."

Karolina looked at Alex for a second and seemed to be classifying him as one of the better examples of the less than intelligent, English idle rich. Indicating just how under-impressed she was, she ignored his attempts to make conversation and instead changed the subject. "I'm actually travelling to Crete to visit the Temple of Knossos. As I said earlier, I have a passion for history and archaeology. I have permission to visit Arthur Evans' excavation of the temple and hopefully work with him for a few weeks."

"I too am going to Knossos," said the slightly built gentleman who had been introduced as Doctor Constantine Papadopoulos. "As is also Lord Thomas, I believe. Perhaps it will be possible that we will be companions to travel?" He seemed to be unaware that his English was not as good as he maybe thought it was.

"I was thinking I might just rent a horse and ride there by myself, but perhaps it would be good to travel as one of a party," said Karolina, smiling at Doctor Constantine and Lord Thomas.

"Oh yes dear!" said Millicent, "I think it would be much better to travel with Lord Thomas than be a young lady travelling on her own."

"I believe that the shipping line has a subsidiary that provides an omnibus once a week, that goes from Chania, to Rethymno, then Knossos before finishing in Heraklion," said Alex. I'm sure the captain would be happy to make arrangements for you . . ."

"Good idea, Alex," said Lord Thomas. "That sounds like just the ticket. Let's see what we can arrange before we get to Chania."

Alex felt a little relieved that he'd finally managed to make an intelligent and helpful contribution to the dinner conversation, without digging a deeper hole than when he'd started. He saw the white jacketed waiters arriving with the fish course and made a resolution that for the rest of the dinner, he would open his mouth again only if it was to insert food, as opposed to his foot.

By the time the desert course of caramel pudding or pineapple royal was being served, Alex felt a little more confident. He'd survived dinner by making only polite unobtrusive conversation, although he felt his less than scintillating conversation had re-enforced Karolina's opinion that he was a good example of an English aristocratic with less than dazzling intelligence.

After everyone had finished eating, Alex kept a careful eye on the captain. When he rose to thank his guests and wish them a good evening, Alex was already prepared and had his walking stick in his hand. Quickly and methodically, he successfully rose from his chair and nodded and smiled at the other guests, including Karolina.

Karolina paused and studied the way in which Alex had been forced to use his walking stick to raise himself from his chair. As he was saying goodnight to the other guests, she studied him thoughtfully for a few seconds.

Sir Alfred and Constantine nodded to each other in some sort of unspoken agreement and left together for the first-class smoking room. Mrs. Webster informed them all loudly that she and her husband were retiring to their 'stateroom' on the upper deck, while Karolina left for her cabin on deck four, the next deck down and on the same deck as Alex's cabin.

Chapter 5

Once the various dinner guests had departed for their different destinations, Alex and Lord Thomas moved to the 1st class salon, for a night cap.

They sat in comfort in the brown, deeply buttoned, leather chesterfield chairs, savouring the aroma and taste of the fine single malt whisky.

Alex asked Lord Thomas a question, "I may be talking out of turn Lord Thomas, but did you notice the young gentleman at the table seated behind me this evening?"

"Please call me just Thomas, Alex" smiled Lord Thomas " . . . or even Tommy if you must!"

Alex smiled back. "Karolina is one in a million isn't she. I have never met so confident a young lady – although I admit that going straight from an all-male boarding school to an all-male university and then straight on into the navy, means that I've met very few young ladies at all."

"How old were you when you volunteered?" asked Lord Thomas

"Twenty," replied Alex. "I joined as an ensign. My father was already in the navy and had been at sea for most of my childhood. In some way joining the navy felt like I was getting closer to him. We did actually get to serve in the Mediterranean at the same time during 1915, but on different ships. Even so, we were lucky enough to see each other several times. In 1916 we were actually also both in Admiral Beatie's fleet in the North Sea, but again on different ships."

"Is he still in the navy?"

"No, he died in the war," Alex replied. He stared thoughtfully into his whisky glass for several seconds.

Trying to change the mood, Lord Thomas said, "You were asking me about the young gentleman at the next table?"

"Yes Lord Thomas. Sorry - Thomas. I noticed him in the mirror on the wall behind where you were sitting. He didn't notice me watching him, but he seemed to spend a long time studying our table. At first, I thought it was Karolina that he was watching," Alex felt himself blushing " . . . but he could have only seen her back. It actually seemed to be someone on your side of the table that he was watching most closely. Maybe Doctor Constantine or yourself, I thought."

"What did he look like?" asked Lord Thomas

"Large, well built, strong fellah. About thirty years old, dark curly hair. Wearing a dinner jacket with an embroidered waist coat."

Lord Thomas thought for a minute and then said, "I think I know the chap you mean. Vasiliki Hasapis. Came on board at Corfu, at the same time as Constantine, Karolina and Mr. and Mrs. Webster. Doesn't talk much to anyone. I think he's part of the late-night card school in the smoking room."

Alex considered Lord Thomas's reply thoughtfully. "Is that where Doctor Constantine and Sir Alfred were off to, after dinner?"

"I suspect they were," replied Lord Thomas. "Bit of a compulsion for some people."

Alex agreed with Lord Thomas, but there had been something surreptitious in the way the young man had been watching their table. He resolved to keep a weather eye open for Mr. Hasapis for the rest of the voyage.

Chapter 6

Next morning, Alex again made his way to breakfast early, feeling much better this morning compared to the day before, benefiting from a better night's sleep. He was pleased to find Dai already there, finishing his breakfast.

"Bora Da, Dai," said Alex

"Bora Da, Alex," Dai replied with a smile and paused with half a sausage on the end of his fork. "Sit you down and get you comfy why don't you, bach."

Alex took the offered seat across from Dai and ordered his coffee and breakfast from the waiter. He paused for a few seconds to weigh Dai up.

"Another later night poker game?"

"You have the truth there," said Dai, looking up and studying Alex's face, before going back to enjoying his breakfast.

"I have a question for you Dai. Was there a gentleman, Vasiliki Hasapis, there last night?"

"Very inquisitive young man you are Alex. In my circles that's not always seen as a good thing."

"And what are your circles Dai?"

"Oh well, this and that, a little import, a little export. As I said yesterday, find items that are in short supply, buy cheap and sell high."

"Not good Welsh coal then I take it, but maybe there's a market for something else that's black . . .?"

Dai's head was down looking at his plate, but at Alex's words, his eye's flicked up under his brows and met Alex's own eyes with a steely gaze. "I have no idea what you mean" said Dai in a flat expressionless voice, while he watched Alex for a response. "Is there something in particular that interests you?"

Alex noticed that the man's cheerful Welsh lilting accent had disappeared and he was aware that he was now talking to someone who now appeared to have a much tougher personality.

"All I'm interested in is a little information – about your fellow poker players. Nothing confidential. Just your observations and opinion."

Dai continued eating his breakfast at a good rate, but was obviously deep in thought about this young man across the table from him. Eventually Dai replied cautiously, as he continued shovelling his breakfast into his mouth. "Well, Vasiliki Hasapis doesn't say much about himself, but he isn't a big poker player, I'm pretty sure about that. Small bets and quick to fold. I'm not sure why he hangs out in the smoking room at all, if it comes to that. I will say however, that in my opinion, I'm not sure I would choose to do business with him. There is something about him that does not inspire my trust in him."

"Do you think he's there in order to watch someone?"

Again, Dai paused for some time before responding with a question for Alex. "Do you think he's with the authorities or something?" said Dai suspiciously. "If he is . . . . "

"No. No. I just wondered if you thought he was watching someone."

"Well, when you play poker, no matter how high or small your bets, you're always watching the other players. But yes, I would say the Vasiliki talked less and watched more than a typical card player."

"He didn't win or lose much then?"

Dai laughed, "Not that I remember. The big loser was Sir Alfred. Same as the night before. That fellah seems to think he's entitled to get the right cards to win no matter how low the odds are."

"Who did he mostly lose to?"

"Constantine, without a doubt. Sir Alfred lost several big games to him after raising the stakes on bad hands. You know, now that you mention it, if Vasiliki was paying attention, he may have heard something of interest last night."

"And what was that?" asked Alex.

"Well Constantine likes his drink and gets very talkative. He told us all that he was on his way to Knossos. His granddaughter, Ariadne, lives there. Constantine's daughter, Ariadne's mother, died recently. Since Ariadne's father died many years ago, Constantine is her last remaining family. So, what he let slip was that he was taking something of great value to Ariadne. That caused everyone around the table to pay attention."

"Any idea what it might be?"

"No. Even though he was in his cups by then, I think he caught himself and realised it might not be a wise to continue with that particular conversational topic."

"So, he won a sizeable sum from Sir Alfred. Did he win money from you too?"

Dai's voice hardened. "That is my personal business. And that would be something you should stay clear of. And it would be in your own interests to do that."

"My apologies Dai. I retract the question."

"That's okay Alex bach" said Dai, placing the last mouthful of breakfast into his mouth. "No offence taken. But thinking about it, if you do find out anything more about Mr Vasiliki, I think I would be interested in that myself. I'd take it as a valuable favour if you would let me know."

"I'll do the best I can Dai."

Nodding, Dai stood up and made his way out of the dining room.

Alex sat at the table, thinking for a while. He decided he had learnt a little more about Vasiliki Hasapis, but much more about Dai and that Dai was a man he would be careful of in the future.

Chapter 7

After breakfast Alex decided that taking more exercise today would help him sleep tonight. Taking his walking stick, he did as many laps of the promenade deck as he could until the pain in his leg told him he needed to stop. He'd noticed the ships library earlier, forward of the promenade deck. Promising himself that he would do some more laps later, he drifted along to it. Since he'd finished the only book he had brought with him, he thought he might find another book to distract him for the rest of the duration of the voyage to Crete. Entering the library he saw the first-class steward, tidying newspapers and magazines from the tables. The room was darkly panelled in wood, with just a little natural light from one large skylight. Additional light came from small table lights on the four small tables, with a bigger reading light over a large inclined newspaper table. Two looming oak bookshelves stood either side of the door. Alex nodded acknowledgment to the steward and started to browse the bookshelf to the left of the entrance door. He found an Arthur Conan Doyle book, "The Poison Belt" that he'd not read before. He was skimming through it to see if it interested him enough to borrow it, when the door opened and Doctor Constantine Papadopoulos entered, dressed in a white linen suit, smoking a tobacco pipe with a short, thick, ornamental bowl. Constantine stopped after crossing the threshold and, without noticing Alex behind the door, called to the steward.

"Dimitrios. Please to answer a question for me."

"Yes sir. What can I do for you sir?" replied the steward.

"I was reading on the promenade deck earlier. While I read, you notice anyone strange hanging around my cabin? Anyone who should not have been here? Maybe another passenger? Maybe another crew member?"

"No sir! Nothing missing I hope sir!"

"No, not missing. Just a few things moved around a little. My case not properly closed. I sure I close it."

"Maybe the maid was tidying up sir?"

"No. Maid not yet been. This just had happened. Never mind. But please to keep an eye open for me, will you?" Constantine slipped the man a couple of coins and left.

Alex raised his eyebrows to Dimitrios and asked, "Is theft much of a problem on the ship?"

Dimitrios expression showed his shock. "No sir! Absolutely not!". He shook his head vigorously. "Very good crew. All very trustworthy. All very keen to not lose their jobs."

"I'm sure they are," Privately he thought that needing their jobs was not always protection against temptation. He was very aware that many of the passengers did not appreciate how the wealth they took for granted and displayed without thought, could be an afront to others living in much less privileged circumstances. Alex smiled at Dimitrios then said, "The gentleman is probably just confused or maybe a little forgetful."

As Alex left the library and crossed the promenade deck, he noticed the man he now knew as Vasiliki watching him carefully but unobtrusively from one of the heavy oak chairs under a sun shade.

Chapter 8

The ship's upper deck held the promenade and sun deck, with comfortable oak reclining chairs and sunshades. On the same deck were the bridge, first-class dining room, salon, smoking room and library. It also held the larger suites and staterooms for some of the wealthier first-class passengers. Other smaller cabins for first-class were below it on deck four. On that deck, cabin doors opened out onto a wide walkway that circumnavigated the ship. Deckchairs were placed at strategic intervals. Sitting on one of a pair of deckchairs outside her cabin, Karolina was wearing a white dropped waist sundress and sunglasses, with a soft wide-brimmed cloche sun hat with a wide red band. She had just placed her book on the table between the chairs and was sipping a coffee, when Constantine approached, in his white linen suit, also carrying a book.

"Good morning my lady," said Constantine "Would it be acceptable to sit down for me?"

"Of course," said Karolina, smiling, removing her hat and pushing her sunglasses up into her blonde hair. "How are you this morning?"

"Very good my lady." He said, "Like you, I wish to enjoy the sun. It is good to my old bones." He lowered himself carefully into the chair next to her. For several minutes they both sat in peaceful silence and Karolina felt herself drifting slowly towards the edge of sleep.

Murder on Crete

Constantine broke the silence. "So tomorrow, we arrive in Kríti. Crete as you call it in your language. And as you told last night at dinner, you also travel then to Knossos?"

"Yes" agreed Karolina. "I will be going to the Arthur Evans dig at Knossos temple."

"It is known to me well. I own large villa in the street of the villa of Arthur Evans. I know much about archaeology because I live so close to Mister Evans and to Knossos. There is much very beautiful archaeology from Crete. You know of jewellery from the times of King Minos. Very beautiful. Very valuable. There are pictures in this book. This book tells everything about Minoan history." Constantine waved the book he was holding.

"I'm afraid I don't know much about jewellery sir. I'm hoping to learn a lot more about Crete and King Minos when I'm in Knossos. Might I see your book?"

Constantine paused and looked cautiously at Karolina, before slowly handing the book to her. Karolina opened the book, bound in lightly tanned leather and glanced at some of the photographic pages in it. Each photographic plate was protected by a thin sheet of tissue paper.

"These are beautiful," she said as she studied the black and white photographs. "It's not a book I've heard of. Do you think I could borrow it for a while?"

Again, Constantine paused before answering. "Perhaps. If you take great care of it. The book is very valuable to my family." Then, he shrugged and handed it over to her.

"I will be very careful with it sir," she said. "Thank you." Karolina began to browse slowly through the book as she continued to speak. "Last night I believe you said you lived in Corfu, not Crete?"

"Yes," replied Constantine. "I have not seen Knossos for many years. In 1906 I left Crete. My daughter and her husband, they stayed living in my villa in Knossos."

"You are going back there to visit them?" asked Karolina

"No. I am sad that they both have died now. My son-in-law he killed in the Balkan war in 1912. My daughter she died last month from attack of the heart."

"I'm so sorry sir. You have my heartfelt sympathy." Karolina was aware as she spoke to Constantine, that a well-built young man with dark curly hair was leaning over the rail a few yards away, staring out to sea but also casting glances towards her. For some reason Karolina had the feeling that he was trying to listen in to their conversation.

"Thank you, my lady. My granddaughter Ariadne is now by herself – but she is seventeen and say she is now the house mistress, but I now will stay with her, or perhaps we both will go back to Corfu together."

"I was engaged at seventeen myself and I thought I was very grown up. My fiancé was a friend of the family and we had known each other since we were small children. My parents always thought, assumed I guess, that we would get married, but he left for the war before we could even set a date and then he died. I wonder now what our life might have been like, or if we were even really in love . . ." Karolina wondered why she was sharing such private thoughts with a stranger, but the thoughts had been swirling around in her mind for months and had bubbled to the surface of their own accord. Maybe she could only say them out loud now, because Doctor Constantine was a stranger, who she would not likely ever meet again. She made a conscious effort to change the subject. "Why did you leave Crete?"

"I am the doctor for Prince George of Greece and Denmark," announced Constantine, puffing his chest out with pride. "Prince George was High Commissioner of Crete and is a very great man and I am his close friend. He has many famous friends who I know well. I am friends with his wife Princess Marie also. She is great friends with Sigmund Freud you know. I have met that great man many, many times. When Prince George was High Commissioner, he did much good for Crete and many liked him, but some were enemies. Soon the enemies became strong and he had to leave Crete. He asked me, his friend and doctor to go with him and his wife."

"Well I'm sure your granddaughter is very much looking forward to seeing you again."

"Yes. And I also am looking forward to seeing her. I have not seen her in too long a time. I would be pleased to introduce to you when we reach Knossos. Her English is very good. I'm sure you will like her. If you are looking to rent a room, she has many in our villa. These she rents to archaeologists. Perhaps you will rent a room from her and my daughter will show you around Knossos temple and Heraklion?"

"I'm sure I will enjoy making her acquaintance Constantine. If I am working on the dig for a couple of weeks, it would be good to rent a room close by and then we will have plenty of time to get to know each other."

"I look forward to it, Miss Karolina." Smiling, he rose and said, "But for now, I need to prepare myself for luncheon." and turning, went back to his cabin, a short distance along the deck.

Karolina picked up the book and began to read the index, before selecting a chapter that looked particularly interesting. She was concentrating on the early origins of the Minoan civilisation on Crete, when a polite cough distracted her. Looking up she saw a short, heavily built middle aged man with dark curly haired smiling down at her.

"Good day Miss Karolina!" said Dai Williams, "My name is Dafydd Williams and very pleased to meet you I am."

"Well, you already seem to know my name, Mr. Williams," said Karolina.

"Please, Dafydd if you will, or better still is Dai, isn't it."

"Dai it is then. Would you like to sit down? . . ."

With a sigh to herself, she put Doctor Constantine's book down on top of her own book and resigned herself to not reading either of them for some time.

Chapter 9

After luncheon, Alex seated himself on the promenade deck with his Sir Arthur Conan Doyle book, but rather than read, he watched a spirited game of quoits between two young couples. He soon spotted Lord Thomas approaching.

Smiling at the older man, Alex asked, "Looking for someone to borrow a cigarette from? I managed to bribe the second-class steward to smuggle a couple of packets to me."

Lord Thomas smiled back. "Not required old chap. I had a word with the chief steward and established my own lines of supply. May I sit down next to you?"

"Of course, sir."

Lord Thomas sank down into the deckchair next to Alex and dropped his own book and a packet of cigarettes on the table next to him.

"Good dinner last night. Enjoyed the food and the conversation. Company was excellent."

"Absolutely, sir. I think Captain Meunier likes to keep a good table. He obviously appreciates good food and wine."

"And what did you think of that Karolina? She certainly has a way of setting you back, when she's so direct and forthright in her opinions. Refreshing, when so many people say one thing when they think another. Put Sir Alfred in his place good and proper! Good looking young woman too," Lord Thomas looked sideways at Alex as he said this.

"Er . . Yes, I suppose you're correct sir," said Alex stuck for words. "I'm afraid I'm not much of a judge, sir. As I mentioned, I was in an all-male boarding school and college and then I joined the navy, so I haven't had the chance to meet many young women."

"Well take my word for it Alex, intelligence, beauty and confidence don't often come along in the same package . . . and if I'm not mistaken, it's coming along again right now."

Much to Alex's discomfort, the object of their discussion came walking along the promenade deck towards them and stopped in front of them.

"Good morning gentlemen. Please don't get up. In fact, if you don't mind, may I sit with you for a few minutes? I'm enjoying being out in this fresh air. Feels absolutely wonderful."

"Alex and I would be delighted if you joined us Karolina" replied Lord Thomas. "In fact, we were just agreeing how much we both enjoyed your company last night."

Karolina turned to look at Alex, who had immediately begun to blush. Deciding to accept the compliment, she smiled at both men and took a deckchair next to Sir Thomas.

"Thank you, Tommy. I enjoyed your company too," acknowledged Karolina.

Lord Thomas smiled happily. "Every time you call me 'Tommy' I feel twenty years younger."

"Oh Tommy, I can see you're no old man. You're still in the prime of life! I suspect many young ladies would be over the moon to have you escort them to a dance!"

"Now I feel about thirty years younger," laughed Lord Thomas, "but I think you're flattering me."

"Not at all Tommy! I know there's still life in the old dog yet!" laughed Karolina

"Well, we will see," said Lord Thomas.

"I hear that after we disembark in Port Chania, you will be travelling on to Knossos?"

"That's true my dear and then I will continue on to Heraklion."

"I was talking to Mrs. Webster, and she, her husband and Sir Alfred are also going to Heraklion. I have agreed to travel with them as far as Knossos. Sir Alfred told me he will be meeting with an American millionaire who has a yacht in the harbour at Heraklion. He said there was sure to be a party and he would invite me along as his guest, but I'm not so sure about that. Mr. and Mrs. Webster are also going on to Heraklion and catching another ship from there to Alexandria and then cruising up the Nile on a dahabiya," said Karolina. "I'm quite jealous, you know. The Pyramids, Thebes, Karnak, Aswan – seems like a dream trip."

"With your interest in archaeology, the idea must be attractive."

"There is that, but also the beauty of those places, not to mention the Nile itself. And the chance to walk in those very same temples where pharaohs walked thousands of years ago. Wouldn't that be wonderful!"

"I see your point and I agree with you, young lady – but I think you may have missed your calling. You should work with the Thomas Cook travel agency. With that enthusiasm, you could fill all the places on all their Nile cruises," said Lord Thomas.

"Well, if the money ever runs out, I'll consider it," said Karolina. "Or maybe I'll just see about a place on one of those cruises for myself"

"I'd love to do that too," said Alex, "Not with you I mean, not that that wouldn't be wonderful too of course, but I didn't mean . . ." As they both turned to look at him, Alex thought to himself, 'stop digging the hole, Alex'. He hastily resorted to every Englishman's number one diversionary conversation topic, "Looks like the weather's deteriorating." At least he hoped that was a safe move.

Karolina seemed to not know how to respond Alex's change of topic, so she turned to Lord Thomas. "Actually Tommy," and she added as an afterthought, "and Alex, I wanted to ask your opinion on something else . . . I've discovered that we also have another fellow compatriot of yours travelling with us – an Englishman called Dafydd Williams? I wondered if you had met him and if so, what do you make of him?"

Alex laughed, "Well one thing is, never let him hear you call him an Englishman! He's Welsh and he's likely to react strongly by explaining to you in detail, at length and with great feeling, the differences between the English and the Welsh."

"I'd agree with Alex," smiled Lord Thomas. If you're not careful, he'd finish his explanation off with a few verses of "Men of Harlech! But other than that, I'm afraid I don't know anything more about him. Why do you ask?"

"Well, he approached me earlier today and questioned me at length about my archaeological work. Eventually, he got round to asking me if I ever came across finds – statues, jewellery, that sort of thing – particularly Egyptian - that might have value. It appears that he is travelling on to Cairo after Crete, to buy those sorts of artefacts and take them back to England. It also sounds like this is not the first time he's done that."

"Really?" said Lord Thomas. "Is that sort of thing readily available in Egypt?"

"Absolutely. Archaeologists traditionally get a half share of their findings and the other half share goes to the Egyptian Antiquities

Service. Artefacts from either share often end up with dealers in places like Cairo. Funding digs is expensive and selling antiquities is one way of funding it. For some it can also be big business. And in addition to the officially recorded finds, there is a lot of unofficial excavation. What amounts to very damaging robbery from the sites, by locals and foreigners alike. You have to remember that even a small find can easily represent a year's salary for a manual labourer."

"I had no idea." Said Lord Thomas.

"I believe there's also a lot of forgery and faking of artefacts?" added Alex.

"Indeed, and I think Mr. Williams was trying to discover if I could be of assistance to him in his business endeavours. Maybe in finding more artefacts for him, or validating artefacts brought to him." said Karolina. "I'm just very unsure of his scruples and the legality of his business?"

Alex though for a few seconds and then said, "For what it's worth, I would steer clear of getting involved. I have no hard facts to back me up, but when I spoke to him, I got a pretty clear signal that during the war he was probably and maybe still is, involved in the black market. Getting hold of expensive artefacts, especially those that he may not have clear title to, sounds right up his street. I also got the feel that if things don't go the way he wants, he's not above applying a little physical persuasion."

Karolina sat thoughtfully for quite some time. Finally looking up she said, "Well, it looks like you may have been right about the weather. The wind has picked up." The clouds were now low and looming, hiding the blue sky. The water had become choppier, with the wind skimming white foam off the tops of the waves. "I suspect we'll be in for a bit of a blow. I hope it won't get too bad,"

"And hopefully it won't slow us down in reaching Chania," said Lord Thomas.

"I hope so too," replied Karolina. "Well, I guess I'll see you both this evening gentlemen, if the weather doesn't get too bad, or, as some might say . . " then changing to a deep, slow, Texas drawl, ". . . If the good Lord be a willin' an' the crick don't rise!"

Karolina, stood and walked away, leaving the two gentleman looking after her, laughing at her comedic goodbye.

As he settled back in his deckchair again, Alex felt a little jealous at the thought of the dashing Sir Alfred travelling to Knossos with the attractive Karolina and perhaps taking her to some ritzy party. He was also suspicious that Sir Alfred's intent was not just to find a convenient way to travel from Chania to Heraklion, but also he wanted to spend more time with Karolina, who he obviously had designs on. Alex wondered if in fact she might be safer traveling on her own, by horse after all.

After talking to Lord Thomas and Alex, Karolina made her way back to her cabin. During her Grand Tour of Europe, she had religiously kept up-to-date with writing frequent letters back to her mother and father and it was time for her to write the next in the series. She enjoyed writing them. People had said that travelling by herself was very brave, but the emotion she felt most frequently was loneliness. The result of not having a someone, a companion, to share the experiences with. In some way, writing about those experiences to her mother and father, made her feel as if they were there with her. That they were sharing her travels. Back in Texas, she had always been able to at least talk to her mother and most of the time her father too, even though, sometimes he had to travel with his oil drilling and exploration work. It was true that she'd made many friends during her travels and she enjoyed their company, but it could never be the same as sharing her thoughts with someone close to her, or people she had known all her life.

In Texas, she had also had Randolph to talk too and she had also known him for almost all her life. But now she looked back on it, he was different to her parents. She had never felt that she could talk to him about anything she wanted to. There had always been a feeling that he saw himself as a man's man and men didn't talk about certain things. The sort of things that she wanted to talk about. She'd found herself accepting those limitations and now she thought about it, she realised that she had been shaping herself to be what he wanted her to be. Perhaps it was also that she was understanding herself better, as she grew older and wiser. After all, she was twenty-three now!

Lying back on her bunk in her cabin, she reached for her pack of blank stationary and started to write, about all her experiences since her last letter and about the people she had met. For some reason she didn't understand, she instinctively decided not to include Alex in the descriptions of new acquaintances in her letter home.

Chapter 10

Before dinner that evening, Alex retired to his cabin on deck four, below the promenade deck. He wanted to get back to the Sir Arthur Conan Doyle book that he had found in the library and contentedly lay back on his bunk, underneath the cabin window, hoping to finish at least another chapter before getting dressed for dinner. He was half way through the chapter, when he heard a loud splash, followed by loud shouts in what he guessed was Greek. The shouts were coming from the walkway outside the cabin. Throwing the book down, he grabbed his stick and went out onto the walkway. In the gloom of early dusk, he could see Vasiliki a few cabins down from him, standing by the handrail, trying to attract attention. When Vasiliki saw Alex, he began to gesture alternately up to the promenade deck, then over the handrail towards the sea, still shouting in Greek.

"What happened?" Alex shouted back as he hobbled towards Vasiliki.

Vasiliki changed to English to reply. He spoke good English with an Oxford accent and only a trace of Greek. "I was leaning on the rail, smoking a cigarette, when a man fell down from the promenade deck above and he fell past me into the water!"

Alex wasted no more time. Taking the few steps back towards his cabin, he grabbed the lifebelt hanging on the wall there. Looking over the handrail, threw the lifebelt as far back into the ships wake as he could. Seeing a crewman arrive at the end of the walkway, Alex shouted to him, "Quickly! Run to the bridge and tell the helmsman that there's a man overboard on the port side. Get the ship turned round." The crewman stopped and hesitated, looking at Alex, undecided. "Quickly man. Get to the bridge!" shouted Alex. Responding to the authority in Alex's voice, the crewman turned and ran down the walkway.

The shouting and running feet had caused several passengers to emerge from their cabins, including Karolina. Seeing Alex with Vasiliki she came up to them. "What's happened? Is there anything I can do?"

"No. Someone's gone overboard. I pitched a lifebelt in as soon as I heard, but at the ships speed it will probably be too far from whoever it is, for him to get to. But it will act as a marker for us to use for where to begin our search." As Alex said this, he was calculating the chances of a successful search. Dusk would rapidly becoming full dark and with the wind kicking up the waves he didn't like the chances. "Regretfully I don't think there is much you can do to help, Karolina. Perhaps it would be best for you to stay in your cabin?"

"If there's going to be a search, I've got as good a pair of eyes as anyone!" Karolina said determinedly.

Alex was surprised to find himself having the completely inappropriate thought that, to him, her eyes were a damn site better than anyone else's on the ship, but then he shook his head to clear the thought and nodded. "You're right. We need to get up on the promenade deck. The extra height will increase how far we can see. It will take about ten minutes for the ship to turn around, but we can be ready to search as soon as the ship has completed the turn." As he said this, the ship began to slow and make a turn to port, heeling over as it did so. "Good, they've put the helm over."

"I will come also!" said Vasiliki, who had been listening to Alex. "I will also help the search."

Together the three of them made their way as quickly as they could towards the companionway. Vasiliki and Karolina led the way, but the sloping deck made it especially difficult for Alex to follow them. They reached the companionway to the promenade deck and began to climb. As they arrived at the top of the stairs, Lord Thomas was standing there. "What's all the fuss!" he demanded.

"Looks like a man overboard, Lord Thomas." said Alex, arriving behind Vasiliki and Karolina. "We're turning around to go back to the search area. It would be a great help if you could get whoever will assist and take a position forward on the other side of the promenade deck and keep your eyes peeled. We should be back at the search area in a few minutes."

"Of course dear boy. I'm on my way!"

Alex watched him walking quickly across the deck and also saw Dai coming back from the stern of the promenade deck, towards Lord Thomas, with an enquiring look on his face.

"Alex, look!" said Karolina and pointed to an object on the deck, by the handrail. It was a tobacco pipe, with a short, thick, ornamental bowl. "I've seen that before!"

"And here also!" exclaimed Vasiliki. He reached down and picked up a pair of gold framed spectacles.

Alex reached out his hand for the spectacles and Vasiliki passed them him. Karolina picked up the tobacco pipe and turned it over, examining it. "I'm afraid I recognise both of these items. I believe they are Doctor Constantine's". Alex looked towards the handrail and pointed to a large smear on the handrail. "If I'm not mistaken, that's blood."

"Maybe he fell and banged his head on the handrail, before falling in the water?" said Vasiliki.

"Yes," replied Alex and paused for a few seconds, thoughtfully. "Yes, it certainly looks like it." He looked up and saw both Karolina and Vasiliki looking at him closely. Over their shoulders he saw Sir Alfred come out of the smoking room and look around. Spotting them standing by the rail, he walked towards them.

As he came closer, he said, "I say. What's all the fuss about?"

"Looks like a man overboard," replied Alex

"Really?" said Sir Alfred and looked over the rail, down into the sea, "Not much chance for the chap is there?"

"We've turned around now. We'll search for him as we retrace our course." said Alex.

"Well, I hope we won't waste too much time on it," said Sir Alfred. "This is going to delay us getting to Crete!"

Karolina was affronted by his callousness. "We need to do all we can if it means possibly saving a human life!"

"Of course, dear lady, of course. Just saying the poor fellah has not got much of a chance. And it is nearly dark now. Perhaps we should retire to the salon for a little refreshment? This sort of thing is best left to the crew. They know what they're doing after all."

"Alex, Vasiliki and I are staying right here. We're going to help in any way we can with the search."

Sir Alfred looked at Alex disapprovingly, but before he could object further, Mr. and Mrs. Webster also arrived.

"Whatever is the matter?" asked Mrs. Webster

"We were just telling Sir Alfred, there's a man overboard," said Karolina

"How terrible! We were in our stateroom and didn't see anything, but we heard the fuss and the shouting. Do you have any idea who it is?"

Alex held up the pipe and spectacles and replied, "Well, we found these items on the deck. We rather think that they belong to Doctor Papadopoulos."

"Really?" said Sir Alfred, "That's interesting!"

"Why is that?" asked Alex.

"Oh, no reason. I just thought it interesting that you worked out who it was so quickly."

More crew and some passengers were now appearing, taking up positions at the handrail along the edges of the promenade deck, and searching the sea. Lord Thomas came back from the forward rail to re-join the little group.

"We have several passengers volunteering to help, together with the crew, but it's really getting too dark to see much."

At that moment, two small searchlights on the forward edge of the promenade lit up, followed quickly by two much larger searchlights on either wing of the bridge. The bright lights began to sweep the sea, but unfortunately, they were only covering a small part of the sea at any one time.

"It will still take several minutes to get back to where the alarm was raised," said Alex to Lord Thomas. Alex signalled to the nearest crewman. "Please present Lieutenant Armstrong's compliments to Captain Meunier and suggest that we point the searchlights up at the low cloud. The light will reflect downwards and cover much more area." The crewman, forgetting for the moment that Alex was only a passenger, instinctively threw Alex a salute and turned, running off to the bridge. Alex noticed Lord Thomas and Karolina looking at him. He shrugged and mumbled, "Navy trick. Learnt it from my old chief petty officer."

As they turned back to the rail, the searchlights swung up to the sky and suddenly the sea was revealed as if lit by bright moonlight. Sir Alfred excused himself on the pretext of escorting Mrs. Webster back to the salon, leaving her husband to help in the search.

Almost immediately, four crewmen ran up and began to clear the rail around one of the life boats. As soon as they had done that, they took to the winches on the davits supporting the lifeboat and began to swing it out.

Vasiliki turned to Alex and asked excitedly, "What's happening! Have they seen the man who fell?"

"I don't think so. It's a standard drill to get a boat ready, just in case the man is spotted. Means they can get to him and get him out the water as quickly as possible."

"Oh." Said Vasiliki and seemed to calm down.

Karolina was alongside Alex at the rail. "Realistically, what do you think Constantine's chances are?" she asked quietly.

"Oh, I'm sure we'll spot him soon," said Alex.

"I'm not a delicate pussytoes!" Karolina said in a low forceful voice. When she saw the puzzled look spreading across his face, she hissed "It's an American flower!" Then, as she saw Alex struggling to hide a grin she hissed at him again, "That's not funny!" but then found she was struggling to hide her own smile. "Well maybe a little bit. But the point is I'm not liable to fall apart in an emergency! Realistically, what are his actual chances?"

Alex looked her in the eyes and studied her expression. Trying to judge just how self-controlled she really was. He was impressed by the way she returned his appraisal with a steady, calm, intelligent gaze. "Realistically? Low. Even in daylight, I'd say we only stand a 25% chance of spotting him and even that only if he is capable of treading water. At night? In a choppy sea? One in a hundred. And he may not be treading water. Odds are that when he fell in and hit the water, he would have gasped for air, but drawn water into his lungs instead and sank. Even if not, the wake from the ship could have pulled him under. No, I think the captain is showing due diligence and doing all the right things, but I think he knows that he will be one passenger short when we make port tomorrow." After a few seconds absorbing his summary Karolina and then Alex turned back to the rail and resumed scanning the sea.

Karolina, Alex and Vasiliki maintained their search in silence for several minutes. Alex broke the silence. "Vasiliki, can you go over what happened again?" said Alex

"Certainly. I wish to help any way I can. Lieutenant Armstrong, I believe? And Miss McAllister also?"

"I'm sorry, yes. I'm afraid I skipped the formalities of introduction given the circumstances."

"No problem old chap. Quite the right thing to do."

"So, can you go over what do you remember about the incident again for me?"

"Of course," said Vasiliki, but he looked carefully at Alex before he continued. "I was enjoying my cigarette, leaning on the handrail, taking in the fresh air, when suddenly a shape fell, almost directly in front of me. He fell from the promenade deck above where I was standing. I believe the gentleman was short and wearing a white linen suit. Not at all suitable for a sea voyage. I didn't actually see his fall into the water, but when I looked over the rail, there was no sign of him."

"But you heard his fall into the water?"

"Oh yes. Made quite a splash don't you know."

"But no shout as he fell?"

"Er…No. I do not think so. No shout that I heard anyway." replied Vasiliki a little uncertainly.

"Interesting," said Alex.

Both Karolina and Vasiliki looked at Alex expectantly, but Alex turned to look thoughtfully out to sea and said nothing more.

About ten minutes later, a shout went up from one of the crew on lookout. And he pointed off to the starboard bow. The crewman at the rail next to him left the rail and ran back to the bridge. Almost immediately the ship slowed to half speed. Alex together with Karolina, Vasiliki and several other passengers moved quickly to the rail by the crewman.

"Just the lifebelt," said Alex. "But at least we know that we're close to where he went in"

"Yes." Said Vasiliki "Let us hope we will find him soon. We must keep looking."

The three of them returned to their station at the rail, in hope, but not in expectation.

Chapter 11

Next morning, Alex and Karolina met by prior agreement at eight o'clock in the dining room for breakfast. The search had continued for three and a half hours, but although they criss-crossed the area, passing the lifebelt that Alex had thrown over the side as a marker several times, no sign of Doctor Constantine Papadopoulos had been spotted. The weather had continued to deteriorate. Eventually it became a light rain that made things worse by severely hampering vision, as well as soaking the searchers. Eventually Alex had insisted Karolina go down to her cabin. Reluctantly she agreed and left Alex at the rail.

Alex was exasperated when she returned a few minutes later wearing a waterproof coat and hat, carrying an additional weatherproof jacket and hood for Alex. When Alex asked where she had found the spare clothing, she said she had requisitioned them from a passing sailor. Alex wondered what the sailor had made of that.

After the search was abandoned, they left the promenade deck had returned to their cabins on the deck below, in a very sombre mood, before agreeing to meet for breakfast and then saying their goodnights.

Now they sat in silence eating breakfast together, until Karolina suddenly challenged Alex. "Why were you questioning Vasiliki!"

Alex paused with a sausage halfway to his mouth and a puzzled look on his face. "I just wanted to go over what he saw again, to get it straight in my head."

"It was more than that! You had something on your mind. Something you were thinking about. What was it?"

"I don't know," said Alex, then paused. "I guess there were a couple of things that didn't gel for me."

"Really? What was it that was worrying you?"

Alex put his knife and fork down and leant back in his chair. "Well. You saw Constantine. What was he? About five foot tall? If someone that short, with that low a centre of gravity, falls against the handrail, maybe even hits their head on it, where would they fall? Over the rail that's nearly as tall as he is? Or back onto the deck?"

Karolina studied Alex for a second or two. "You said a couple of things were worrying you. What else?"

"Well, that's why I had Vasiliki go over what happened again. He heard the splash as Constantine hit the water. For what it's worth, so did I. But neither of us heard a scream. The promenade deck is forty or fifty feet above the waterline. I can guarantee to you that if I fell that distance, you'd hear me screaming all the way down!"

Karolina nodded "Me too! So, what do you think that means?"

"I'm not sure. Maybe the doctor did hit his head and was unconscious as he fell . . . "

"But then how did he get over the rail? You think he was pushed, don't you?"

"I don't know. I'm not sure."

"Alex. Some advice. Never play poker with me. I can see you are worried, but it's not because you don't know what might have happened. You're worried because you do think you know what happened."

Alex smiled. "I thought all Americans thought all Englishmen were po-faced?"

Karolina laughed out loud. "I'm not sure what you think po-faced means! To an American it means a long face, miserable, no fun! While it might be a common description of the English male for a lot of Americans, I don't think that's what you meant?"

Alex started to blush. "No. I thought it meant poker-faced. I guess the old saying that we English have 'everything in common with America, except, of course, language' must be true", mumbled Alex, embarrassed.

"I'm sorry. I shouldn't make fun of you. I've been tripped up several times by not understanding that the same word can often mean different things in our two languages. I'm trying really hard to remember to always use the word 'trousers' rather than my own word for that same item of clothing!"

Alex relaxed again and realised that Karolina was one of the few girls he had come across who he could enjoy talking too. Even so, he found he could still also say things that just didn't come out as he intended.

"Alex. You've changed the subject. I still think you're worried because you know more about what happened than you want to tell me. Don't go underestimating me," Karolina warned him.

One thing Alex knew for sure was that he didn't underestimate Karolina's abilities. He decided to trust her with his thoughts. "I think Constantine was knocked unconscious, then thrown overboard." Alex looked for an expression of shock on Karolina's face, but she just nodded in agreement. "You were thinking that before I said anything, weren't you!"

"I think I was uncertain about it," said Karolina, "but that could explain what happened. Your logic about his height and why we heard no screams, makes a lot of sense to me. So, what do we do about it?"

"I'm going to see Captain Meunier. I think he should know my suspicions. He'll have to report the incident anyway, when we arrive in Chania tonight. I think he also needs to know that a crime may have been committed aboard his ship."

"Good." Said Karolina, pushing back her plate. As one of my famous American compatriots once said 'Well done is better than well said!' So let's get moving!". She rose and made her way briskly toward the door.

Alex muttered quietly to himself, "I think one of my British compatriots would have said 'let the poor man finish his breakfast first and then get moving' but then again no one asked me." He grabbed one of his pieces of toast in his right hand and, reluctantly leaving the best part of his breakfast to be thrown away, he levered himself up, grabbed his walking stick in his other hand and followed Karolina. "Hold on! Just a second! He shouted after her, "I said *I'd* go to see the captain, not that **we'd** go to see him!

Chapter 12

Captain Francois Meunier looked sternly at Alex.

Karolina had walked onto the bridge without hesitation and full of confidence. The ship's first officer had turned to her in surprise and tried to explain that passengers were not allowed uninvited on the bridge, because they may cause a distraction. She had certainly distracted the helmsman and the other, very young officer, from both of their activities. Alex had a feeling that they would both soon be hearing from the first officer about the importance of discipline and the need to constantly pay attention to their duties. Alex had explained to the first officer that they were there to speak to the captain and Captain Meunier had smiled and waved the first officer back to the binnacle where he had been stood before Karolina's entrance.

Moving to the end of the bridge, Alex had begun to talk to Captain Meunier, with Karolina watching closely, in case he missed out anything important.

After Alex had explained his concerns, Captain Meunier had stroked his moustache slowly. "But mon ami, your suspicions have no evidence! You know as well as I do my friend that at sea many accidents happen that afterwards are most difficult to explain. Le Docteur may have reached beyond the rail and overbalanced. He may have fainted and not cried out. He may have experienced mal de mer! But I understand your concern. When we arrive in Chania, I will personally make sure that the report is taken most seriously and the Greek police will be asked to investigate."

"Thank you, my friend. But if we are to take this incident, as you say, most seriously, then could I ask one favour of you?"

"Of course, my friend," replied the captain, smiling. "What may I do?"

"Could I look at Doctor Papadopoulos's cabin? There may be something there that will provide better evidence for you, that perhaps it was not the accidental fall that you think it was?"

"Oui." said the captain seriously. "Please go to his cabin now and I will send monsieur ensign Arsenault to get the key for you, as he has been most assiduous in listening to our conversation, instead of his taking care of his actual duties!" Captain Meunier unexpectedly turned and made the youngest officer, who had indeed been listening closely to the conversation, jump in embarrassment. Alex smiled. He well remembered from his time in the navy, the almost magical power that captains had, of knowing exactly what was going on behind their backs.

Chapter 13

The young French ensign must have run all the way from the bridge to the purser's office and then back to Doctor Constantine's cabin. Alex and Karolina were waiting on the walkway outside the cabin, which was only a few doors away from their two cabins. The young officer came running up breathlessly to the pair and proudly handed the key to Karolina. Alex smiled and looked at the young officer carefully, noting that he was really no more than a boy of about fifteen. "Tell me," said Alex, "I thought 'Ensign' was only a naval rank, I wasn't aware that it could be found on a passenger vessel?"

"You are correct sir. It is my uncle's little joke to call me ensign, he says I remind him of himself when he was ensign in French navy." He shrugged his shoulders in a very French way, smiled once more at Karolina and walked off towards the companionway, to resume his bridge duties.

Karolina, unlocked the door to the cabin and walked in. The cabin was identical in layout to both of their cabins. A single bunk was against the wall under the window that looked out over the walkway. A bedside table was next to the bunk. Across the other wall was a small chest of drawers with a mirror above it, a wardrobe with a single door and a wooden luggage stand, currently supporting a large suitcase and a smaller attaché case.

Alex stood next to Karolina in the doorway studying the room.

"Where do we start?" asked Karolina.

"Just standing here, do you notice anything?"

Karolina studied the room again. The bed was neatly made, there were the usual toiletries tidily lined up on the chest of drawers. Everything seemed in place, nothing suspicious. "Well, no rare brands of cigar, with unusual shades of lipstick on the end, left in the ashtray!"

Alex smiled. "I am actually reading a book by Sir Arthur Conan Doyle at the moment, so that would have been very appropriate." He walked over to the suitcases on the stand. Turning the attaché case around, he opened the catches and lifted the lid. Inside were some business documents including a small stack of business cards, an envelope hand addressed to Doctor Constantine Papadopoulos at an address in Corfu and a passport. Karolina came across and stood at Alex's shoulder looking down into the attaché case. Alex suddenly became very conscious of how close she was. If he turned his head towards her, his face would be only inches from hers. With an effort, he focused back on the case's contents. He picked up one of the business cards and showed it to Karolina. It proclaimed that Constantine was the owner of Theocaltis Pharmaceutical Laboratory in Corfu. He opened the passport and confirmed the name shown was Constantine Papadopoulos before passing it to Karolina to examine. She double-checked the name in it, then she passed it back to Alex. "I should give this to the captain later," he said and placed it in his pocket. He opened the letter addressed to Constantine, but was disappointed to see it was in Greek.

"From his granddaughter," said both Alex and Karolina together as they saw the signature, and both laughed.

"We need to sort out which one of us is Holmes and which one is Watson." said Alex.

"Well, I refuse to wear one of those silly deerstalker hats, or smoke a briar pipe, so I guess that makes me Watson."

"Oh no. I think you're a better fit for Irene Adler"

"Careful Lieutenant Armstrong! What are you implying? I believe Irene Adler was described as an adventuress and courtesan!"

"Oh no! No! I didn't mean . . . I was just saying . . . Watson was a man and Irene was a very beautiful . . . I mean . . . " Oh damn thought Alex.

"It's OK Alex," said Karolina, "I was just teasing you. I don't mind being Irene Adler. That's better than being either Sherlock Holmes or Watson."

"Thank you. I didn't mean to . . . Well, you know . . ." Alex decided to drop the subject and move on. "Do you notice anything unusual?"

"No. Not really. No cash or wallet, but that could have gone over the side with him."

"The only thing I noticed was the hinge of the case was facing in towards the room, as it is on the suitcase below. I had to turn the case around to open it."

"What does that mean?"

"Probably nothing, but in my room, I have my cases with the hinge furthest away from me, so I can open the lid and get at things easily. Maybe someone moved the cases to look in them, then put them back the wrong way round?"

"That's pretty thin evidence."

"Agreed. Let's check the suitcase." Alex placed the attaché case on the floor, then lifted the suitcase onto the bed and opened it. The clothes inside were screwed up, as if having been bundled hurriedly into the case.

"Okay," said Karolina grudgingly, "You've made you point Sherlock. Pretty impressive actually. So, someone searched Constantine's luggage?"

"I think it may have been the second time it was searched. I overheard Constantine talking to the steward the other day and he seemed to suspect his cabin had been searched back then. It looks like whoever did it may have been interrupted and came back to finish the job."

Alex looked thoughtfully around the room. "There's something else as well. Often, it's more difficult to see something that's not there."

Karolina looked puzzled "I don't understand what you mean."

"The bedside light. It just has the bare bulb. No shade. In my cabin the bedside light has a glass shade decorated with engraved with roses."

"My cabin too – except I think you might find they are foxgloves and daisies."

"I bow to your superior knowledge of botany – foxgloves and daisies it is. But the point is that the shade is missing. Alex bent down and knelt on the floor, looking around the bottom of the bedside table and under the bed. "Ah ha!" he said as he lifted up a fragment of glass that had been lying between the bedside table and the wall. "I could be wrong, but I think there's blood on it!"

"So what does that mean? said Karolina. "Some sort of struggle. Someone fell against the lamp and broke the shade? Perhaps Constantine interrupted someone searching the cabin?"

"And someone then tidied up the room, removing the evidence of what had happened," said Alex.

"But was that someone Constantine, or the interloper?"

Alex was standing again, looking around the room and then more closely at the bed. He flipped the top pillow back, revealing the second pillow beneath it. "Again, what's not here that should be here?"

"The second pillow case!" exclaimed Karolina.

"Very handy if you wanted to wipe up any traces of blood. Then simply drop it overboard."

"It's still very circumstantial, but it does fit together and makes a story that I don't like the sound of. Who do you suspect?"

Alex paused for thought. "Well, Lord Thomas was on the promenade deck when Constantine went overboard."

"Oh, I can't imagine Tommy would ever resort to violence," said Karolina.

"Depends on the provocation." said Alex. "I came across a lot of men who may have never raised a hand in violence before the war, but who ended up as ruthless killers by the time the war ended. It all depends on motivation."

"But I still don't see him having any motivation. I think whoever searched the cabin was looking for something valuable. Tommy has no need to steal money."

"Maybe so, at least not that we're aware of, but I agree that Lord Thomas would be at the bottom of my list. Especially since if money is the motive, there is a better suspect. I have it on good authority that Sir Alfred lost a pretty penny to Constantine playing poker in the smoking room."

"Anyone who bets large amounts of money, on a steamship, with strangers, seems to have a problem. At least in my opinion," said Karolina. "And he makes me shiver when he leers at me."

Alex felt unjustifiably happy that Karolina did not appreciate Sir Alfred's attentions.

"How do you know about his gambling? Were you playing cards with him?" said Karolina in a slightly worried tone, hoping she hadn't inadvertently criticised both Sir Alfred and Alex at the same time.

"Oh no. Never play cards. Certainly not for money." said Alex "Well apart from Christmas that is and then only for a few pennies, you know. No, I was told about it by Dai. He's the one who plays poker."

Karolina looked thoughtful. "He was on the promenade deck too, wasn't he? You also suggested to me that he might be a bit of a tough guy, one of your English, I'm sorry I mean Welsh, gangsters so to speak."

"Maybe. He also said that Constantine drank a little too much and let slip that he was carrying something valuable to give to his granddaughter."

"So, there's the motive then. Either money or something valuable. But something valuable could mean anything. Even a sheet of paper, or a piece of information, can have great value to the right person. Who else do you suspect? Who else was on the promenade deck? "

"Well. Mr. and Mrs. Roberts were in their stateroom, which is just off the promenade deck, or so they say. They turned up pretty quickly after we arrived."

"Surely they couldn't have pushed Constantine overboard?"

"I doubt it and I know of no motive for them." Alex looked questioningly at Karolina, but she shook her head. "They were in the right place at the right time though, so I wouldn't rule them completely out of the picture."

Karolina summed up their discussion. "So, we're not short of people who could have been in the right place at the right time and some also have possible motives. I think we need to keep our eyes open, but not share our suspicions with anyone else. I love the Mediterranean, but if we upset the wrong person, I don't fancy taking an unexpected dive into it from the promenade deck. We should share our suspicions with the police and just the police, when we arrive in Chania."

"Agreed." said Alex. "Let's leave the cabin as we found it and lock it up. I'm going to get a coffee and a bite to eat. Would you fancy something?"

"I'm surprised you can eat anything so soon after that big breakfast you had, but yes, I'll come and have a coffee with you." Leaving the cabin, she locked the door behind them. Smiling to his intense pleasure she then looped her arm in Alex's and they walked slowly off.

Chapter 14

That evening, the approach to Chania was stunning. In the early dusk, the bare, stoney mountains behind the port were a deep purple, capped by pristine white snow. The low-slung bulk of the old fortress to the right and west of the port, dominated the harbour protectively, but it was largely dark. The sun was setting over the Mediterranean further to the west and beyond the headland. To the left of the port was the ancient mosque, practically sitting on the dockside and like the fortress, quite dark. Between the two, the Venetian harbour itself however was already sparkling with lights from the small shops and tavernas strung out, side-by-side, along the ancient quay.

Alex had watched from the promenade deck as the ship approached the port. He continued watching as they moored safely alongside quay. Not long after the ship was secure, the gangway was pushed across and dock workers and crew started to pass backwards and forwards. After a few minutes, two Greek police officers came up the gangway and boarded. Alex turned and made his way to the bridge. Running up behind him came Karolina.

"I see the police have arrived." said Karolina.

"Yes," replied Alex. "I'm on my way to the bridge."

"You're going to tell them that Doctor Papadopoulos was murdered?"

"Well, I'll tell them the evidence we found and what our suspicions are."

"If you think he was murdered, you have to insist that they investigate!"

As they arrived at the bridge, Alex turned and said, "I'm not sure how effective that would be. Government officials don't like to be told what to do and with the police that's especially so." Opening the door to the bridge, Alex was about to enter when Karolina stepped through ahead of him. He saw Captain Meunier talking to the two policemen. One was tall and heavily built, with dark curly hair and bushy eyebrows. He was wearing a dark blue uniform, with a holstered pistol strapped to his waist. He stood silently and a little behind an officer who was clearly the senior of the two policemen. He was wearing a much grander uniform, with gold epaulettes and a cap with copious amounts of gold braid. He also had a holstered pistol at his waist. Alex attracted Captain Meunier's attention and asked, "Permission to come on the bridge, captain?"

"Certainment, mon ami." Turning to the senior police officer, Captain Meunier said, "Please let me introduce Lieutenant Armstrong and Miss McAllister who have taken an interest in the incident involving poor Doctor Papadopoulos. This is Captain Nikolaou of the Chania port police."

Captain Nikolaou turned and looked Alex up and down, then glanced at Karolina, before turning back to Captain Meunier. "This Doctor Papadopoulos – you have his passport I take it?"

"Yes Captain. Here it is," said Captain Meunier handing it to the police officer.

Without saying anything, Captain Nikolaou glanced at the passport long enough to establish the name and then nodded. "Good. This and your statement will be adequate."

"Are you not going to look at the evidence we found in his cabin?" exclaimed Karolina.

"Evidence of what Miss McAllister?"

"Evidence of murder!"

The police officer stared at Karolina. "Murder? That is a very serious allegation. What is this evidence you speak of?"

"When we examined his cabin after he fell overboard, there were signs of a struggle," said Alex.

"Signs? What signs do you mean?"

"The lampshade had been broken and the pieces hidden and his luggage had been searched!" said Karolina.

Captain Nikolaou shrugged. "Lampshades get broken all the time. A passenger might break a lampshade and throw away the pieces so as not to have to compensate the company. How do you know his luggage was searched?"

"Everything had been taken out and shoved back into his suitcase!"

"Regretfully miss, many men are not as tidy as you women would like us to be," shrugged the police officer, smiling at Captain Meunier. "This matter is complete. Thank you, Captain."

"You can't just leave without at least considering the evidence and questioning the suspects!"

"You are wrong miss! I leave when I say I leave, not when you tell me I can! There is no evidence. There is no murder and therefore there are no suspects. The incident was clearly an unfortunate accident and I will not waste any more time listening to your fanciful stories. The matter is closed. Good day." Turning to Captain Meunier he gave a short nod, then he turned on his heel and snapped a command at his junior officer and they both marched stiffly from the bridge.

Captain Meunier shrugged and looked at Alex and Karolina, "I am afraid that some officials are not as conscientious as others, mademoiselle."

"Bloody minded, stubborn and lazy would be closer to the mark!" snapped Karolina.

"Officialdom can be bureaucratic sometimes and you have to approach them tactfully," said Alex.

"Are you trying to say I wasn't tactful? He wasn't going to listen, no matter what I said. And you were no damn use either," Karolina snapped. "Where were you when I was trying to convince mister oh so official capitaine to take action?"

Alex struggled to find a reply, but was saved the trouble since Karolina swirled round and marched out of the bridge. Eventually he turned and appealed to Captain Meunier, "I couldn't get a word in edgeways!"

"Mon ami, such is the role of men when women argue. To say nothing and suffer, or to speak and still suffer. I think mademoiselle Karolina will quickly calm down, but for the sake of Captain Nikolaou, I hope he will not cross swords with her again soon. I fear he may not escape so lightly!"

Alex shook his head. Women had always been a mystery to him. It seemed like the few young ladies who had shown any interest in his company had all ended up being annoyed by him. He couldn't understand it, when all he'd ever tried to do was to be scrupulously polite to them. How could being polite to beautiful young ladies possibly annoy them? He would never understand . . .

Chapter 15

Later that evening Alex was leaning against the rail next to the gang plank, ready to disembark. Earlier, he'd ensured his luggage was packed and already in the hands of the first-class steward, ready to be taken ashore. Captain Meunier approached and stood next to him with both hands on the rail.

"I am sorry that the police were so brusque earlier, mon ami."

"It's okay, Francois. To be honest, I didn't expect a much better response."

"If you are not unhappy, then I have a small favour to ask of you . . . " said Captain Meunier.

"Go ahead Francois. What can I do for you?"

"Well, perhaps not so small a favour. Normally it would be for me to pack up the luggage of Doctor Papadopoulos and hand it over to the police. Then his family must arrange for it to be collected from them. When I spoke to the police, I explained that Doctor Papadopoulos had a ticket including travel on our land transport subsidiary to Knossos. I explained that he has no family but only his young granddaughter. I asked if it would be acceptable for the company, that is for me, to arrange for his luggage to continue to his granddaughter in Knossos, and they agreed." Captain Meunier paused.

"Go on," said Alex

"You have taken an interest in this incident and I know you believe that Doctor Papadopoulos was carrying something of value to his granddaughter. Would you accompany his luggage and deliver it safely and with my condolences to this granddaughter?"

Murder on Crete

Captain Meunier paused again, to let Alex consider, then said "As the ship has been delayed by the search for Doctor Papadopoulos, I have arranged for all first-class passengers to stay in the Kasteli Inn and for the transportation to Knossos and Heraklion to now leave tomorrow morning. I will of course bring the luggage to you and provide your ticket, if you will escort the luggage to Knossos and return here the following day."

Alex looked down at the quay, without actually seeing what was in front of his eyes, thinking of the young girl who had lost her grandfather and who was now alone. Alex turned to Captain Meunier and offered his hand. "Agreed, Francois. I think it's the right thing to do."

Captain Meunier smiled and happily took Alex's hand and shook it. "Thank you, Alex. I will send a telegram to the granddaughter to let her know you are coming. Also, I think I might mention that Miss McAllister has changed her plans to go on horseback to Knossos and will also now be travelling by our transport with you." Captain Meunier's smile grew broader as he saw the red blush begin to spread across Alex's cheeks. "Bon chance! Alex!" he said as he turned and left Alex at the rail.

Alex stayed at the rail looking down on the dock, as he mentally rearranged his plans for the next two days. A few minutes later, Karolina came and leant upon the rail next to him. Alex turned his head and glanced at her. He wondered just how mad at him she was now, after his lack of support against the bureaucratic police officer. Then he quickly turned back to look at the quayside, before she could see him looking at her.

"This is beautiful, isn't it?" she said smiling "So much colour, so exciting."

The friendliness of her greeting took Alex by surprise. He had hardly expected her to talk to him at all and it left him struggling to reply. "Er. . . Yes. Beautiful." he agreed.

"Look at the old men sat outside the bars, playing cards. Do you think it's poker? My father taught me and it might be fun to sit in on a game?"

"I don't think they're playing cards. I think they might be playing backgammon. Very ancient game. I think it goes back to Alexander the Great. Very popular in the ports and towns around the Mediterranean. But probably not a good idea for a visitor to join in, not if you want to hold on to your money," he said with a smile.

"Oh I don't know. Didn't someone once say the important thing is not the winning, but the taking part?"

Alex laughed, "They did, but that was about the Olympics. I think the winning is rather the point in poker or backgammon."

Karolina smiled and they both continued to lean on the rail watching the activities on the quay without comment.

Alex broke the silence, when he said quietly, "I was sorry to hear about your fiancé."

"Thank you," said Karolina. "His name was Randolph. We had been friends since we were little kids. It hit me hard." She lapsed into thought for a while, before continuing. "You know it was strange. We all knew there was a risk to him joining up and going overseas, but none of us really thought anything would actually happen. I can remember my first reaction when I heard. It was surprise, followed by disbelief. It was only after that, that the grief hit me like a locomotive."

"He died from the flu?"

"He did. It took him quickly and the telegram said he didn't suffer."

Alex suspected that may not have been the full story. From bitter experience he knew that many families in the war had been told their loved one's had died quickly and painlessly when the truth had been very different. "You have my sympathy Karolina," he said. "I suppose your parents were upset as well?"

"Yes. Pa wouldn't talk about it for about week or more, spent a lot of time out, riding round the ranch by himself. Pa had thought of Randolph like a son. It hit him hard. Mother loved him too, but she had me to look after. That seemed to help her. But she still keeps saying things like, 'Randolph would have done this, or, Randolph would have liked that'. It seems like she's still keeping him alive in her head. I think that may be a nice thing to do. She's reliving happy memories of him."

"So, was Randolph's death the reason why you came on this trip? You wanted to get away from things that reminded you about him?"

"I think I thought it was time for a change anyway. I wanted to get away and experience new things and go places that I'd read about in books. I guess before Randolph's death I had assumed I would marry him and live on his ranch in Texas and never go those places, but then suddenly I realised nothing was stopping me. It was just up to me. I could travel if I wanted it enough. Nothing was stopping me from seeing those wonderful places."

"And have you?"

Karolina laughed. "Absolutely! I never understood there was so much more of the world than the little I knew about. It was out there all this time, just waiting for me to come and see it!"

"And what will you do next, after Knossos?"

"I really don't know. It's an incredible luxury to aim for a place, get there, then stay as long as you want, or move on when you're ready for some new place. Maybe I'll go to Egypt, or Mesopotamia, or Scotland!" she laughed. "I don't know and I'm enjoying not knowing."

Just then Lord Thomas also came up and stood next to them. "Are you young people ready to disembark, or are you going to lean on that rail all day?"

"Absolutely ready sir. Luggage went down a few minutes ago. Captain Meunier said that transport to the inn would be waiting on the other side of the customs shed. I thought I would just wait for you."

"Well jolly good. Let's shake a leg!"

Karolina looked at him for a few seconds, a little puzzled by the expression, but stood back from the rail ready to follow Alex. Alex picked up his walking stick and began to move towards the gang plank. As he stepped off the deck and onto the gangway, his injured leg failed to lift high enough and caught the raised edge of the gangway. He stumbled forward, dropping his stick. He only stopped himself from falling by grabbing the rail of the gangway. Karolina jumped forward and grabbed his other arm before trying to reach down to pick up his stick from where it had fallen. "Alex, are you OK? Can I help you?"

Murder on Crete

Alex grabbed the stick before she could reach it and pushing up on it, straightened up. Still a little shaken by the fall, he grated out a reply. "I'm okay. I'm fine. I don't need any help." Without looking up at her, he turned his back on her and began to limp down the gangway as fast as he could.

Karolina, paused and looked back at Lord Thomas for guidance. He shook his head and gestured for her to go ahead of him.

The customs shed was small and basic, but brightly lit by flickering carbon arc lamps. Two customs officers each stood behind a table with a pile of luggage to the side of them. As he approached the second table. Alex saw Sir Frederick already at the other table, in a somewhat heated conversation with his customs official. "You damn well don't need to open them!" he was shouting. "They are my personal possessions. That's all you need to know!" The customs officer had one of several large boxes on his table and was determinedly gesturing to one of the dock labourers to open it. The dock worker inserted a crowbar under the lid of the box and pushed down. He lifted the lid away and the customs officer removed an old oil painting wrapped in sackcloth. The painting was of a noble looking horse standing in front of a grand manor house. "If any of these paintings have been damaged, I will have the British Embassy ensure you pay for it!" shouted Sir Alfred.

Alex turned back to the second customs officer and handed over his passport. The officer nodded and called out Alex's name to another dock worker, who found Alex's luggage in the pile and brought it to the table. Opening both cases, the official made a cursory examination of the contents, then nodded again to Alex and closed the cases. He opened Alex's passport and checked through the pages. Satisfied, he picked up a hand stamp and with the other hand opened the passport. With quick hand movements, he stamped the hand stamp onto an ink pad, then on the passport, then back onto the ink pad. Taking a piece of white chalk, he made a cross on the outside of each case and signalled to another worker, standing by with a large two wheeled cart. The man came over and loaded Alex's luggage onto the cart. Alex followed the porter as he pushed the cart towards the large double doors at the far end of the customs shed. Outside the shed he came across Mr. and Mrs Webster, standing with Dai Williams and Vasiliki Hasapis, next to a four wheeled flatbed cart with a skinny, undernourished brown horse between the shafts. The labourer in charge of Alex's luggage carelessly threw it onto the cart with the other passengers' luggage. Alex politely tipped the labourer a few coins.

As he turned back to check on Karolina and Lord Thomas, he saw Captain Meunier walking towards him, accompanied by one of his crew pushing a two wheeled cart loaded with luggage. Behind the captain came an irritated Sir Alfred with a similar cart pushed by another struggling labourer.

When Captain Meunier reached the group, he greeted Alex and shook his hand before saying, "Thank you once more for agreeing to escort the luggage of Doctor Papadopoulos to his granddaughter." The crewman took the suitcase and attaché case from the cart and placed them next to Alex's luggage. Then he turned and hoisted the remaining large wooden trunk from the cart and also slid that onto the flatbed, next to Alex's luggage.

"What's this extra trunk?" asked Alex.

"It is the trunk of Doctor Papadopoulos that he had placed in the cargo hold." said the captain. "It is okay, I hope?"

"Of course." said Alex, looking at the trunk thoughtfully and with interest. "Happy to oblige."

Captain Meunier stepped forward and embraced Alex, wrapping his arms around him and pounding him on the back. "It has been so good to see you again, my friend. I hope your travels are safe and I get the chance to see you again soon." Saying this he kissed Alex on each cheek and hugged him to his chest.

"Er. . . Yes, Er . . soon. That would be very nice," said Alex and placing his hands on Captain Meunier's shoulders, gently regained a little more conservative distance between the two of them. "It really has been good to see you again," said Alex with a grin. He shook his hand again before the captain finally left to return to the ship.

Karolina and Lord Thomas had passed through customs fairly quickly and had now caught up with Sir Alfred as they all arrived at the horse and cart. Karolina caught Alex's attention and rolled her eyes upwards, then gave a slight nod towards Sir Alfred. It looked to Alex like she had something more that she wanted to say, but wanted to save it until they could have a private conversation. This was confirmed when Karolina whispered, "Tell you all about it later," to Alex.

Once all the luggage was loaded the carter flicked his whip across the horse's hind quarters and tugged the bridle until the horse laboriously got the cart into motion. Dai Williams said with a laugh "We were told the hotel is only a few yards away and we're to follow the cart to get to it. This should be good!" He laughed again and started to follow the cart.

"This is outrageous!" exclaimed Sir Alfred. "There should be transport provided, at least for the ladies." he said, turning to smile and nod ingratiatingly towards Karolina and Mrs. Webster.

As they moved off, Alex moved towards Karolina to walk next to her, but Sir Alfred slid in between them to take up position between them. He began to smile and lean in towards her, trying to get her into conversation with him, as they walked down the narrow streets towards the hotel. At first Alex was annoyed that Sir Alfred had so easily out-manoeuvred him into a side-line position, but he soon cheered up when Sir Alfred, leaning in towards and focused on Karolina, didn't notice that the cart horse had decided to lighten his own load. Sir Alfred stepped directly into a sizeable horse pat before realising it. Trying to both continue to charm Karolina while simultaneously shaking off the worst of the mess from his shoe, all without being noticed, he made an amusing sight to both Alex and the passers-by, as the little parade worked its way through the town.

As they moved further away from the custom shed, the narrow streets became lined with shops, cheek by jowl on either side. Even at this late hour, the shop owners greeted the travellers from their doorways, trying hopefully to attract them by displaying their goods for sale to the travellers.

It didn't take the procession long at all to reach the hotel, as it really was only eighty to a hundred yards or so away. The strange little parade arrived at the hotel in just a few minutes. It was an old building, with a stucco frontage of about twenty or twenty-five yards. Shops touched the hotel building on one side and a narrow alley ran down the other side of the hotel. Centred on the building's frontage was a large archway. It covered a shallow recess that contained a pair of dark brown oak, double doors. The doors were now wide open. The travellers had soon crossed the threshold and were now congregating in the main reception area. A cheerful, completely bald, middle-aged man and a young teenage girl with beautiful, long, dark hair, were bustling about the reception area getting the guests to sign the register and handing out keys and instructions. After both Alex and Karolina had been given heavy keys with large wooden tags, Karolina stood by Alex and whispered, "I have some more information. Can we talk?"

"Of course." replied Alex, while keeping his attention on his and Constantine's luggage. "Let me get all this luggage locked in my room and I'll see you back here."

Karolina and the teenage girl soon disappeared up the stairway with Karolina's luggage. Alex had more trouble getting the owner to realise that Alex would not allow Constantine's trunk to be stored next to the reception desk until the morning. Eventually, the problem was solved by the carter, who grumpily agreed to carry the trunk down the ground floor corridor to Alex's room, accompanied by Alex. Alex made sure to tip the carter well for his trouble and the man immediately perked up and broke out into smiles, chatting happily in Greek to Alex, before he left him in the room. Minutes later he was back with the rest of Alex's luggage and this time waved away the offer of more money as he left.

Alex studied the trunk carefully for a minute. Then, removing his tie, he draped it across the lid. He made carful note of where the tie crossed the brass bands of the trunk. He was sure he would be able to tell if the room was broken into and the trunk searched. Before leaving the room, he studied the door lock and was reassured to see it was quite modern and sturdy. Making sure the door locked securely behind him, he made his way back to reception to meet with Karolina.

Chapter 16

Karolina was waiting for him in the reception area, chatting happily with the teenage girl. As Alex entered, Karolina turned to him and said, "I'm told we can go into the lounge to talk. There's no one else in there at the moment." The girl led the two of them into the lounge and they seated themselves at a small table in the window looking out onto the dark little street. The young girl departed. "She's gone to get her father to bring us a couple of drinks."

Sitting across from Karolina, Alex had a chance to study her closely as she looked out the window, watching the people passing by in the street. Her blonde hair was loose and silky, cut in a fashionable bob that Alex recognised was popular with some of the stars in the silent movies. She had strong high cheekbones, but Alex thought her most attractive feature was her startling blue eyes.

"Seen enough?" asked Karolina.

"What? Oh, sorry. I wasn't staring. Well I was but I mean I didn't . . . oh what the heck!" Alex realised that while he had been watching her, she must have been watching him in the reflection in the window.

"It's okay, relax. I'm teasing you. A girl likes to know that she's easy on the eye!"

"Really? I thought it was rude to stare at beautiful . . . I mean, stare at any young ladies?"

"Well I guess it depends on the gentleman who does the staring." She laughed. "I've decided you're harmless, so feel free to stare!"

Murder on Crete

Alex felt a little affronted that she thought he was harmless, but compensated himself by deciding that she must see him as a friend, rather than some bounder that was chasing after her. "Do you get a lot of men staring at you?" he asked, before realising he should have kept his mouth shut.

She looked thoughtful for a minute. "Well, I guess I get my fair share I suppose, but if I'm honest, I think it's because an American and a girl at that, is still a rarity in Europe. I think most Europeans have only seen us American girls in the movies."

"Absolutely!" said Alex, thinking that the comparison to American female movie stars was just right. Then he realised that maybe he shouldn't have agreed quite so enthusiastically. Best change the subject again. "You said earlier that you left home because you needed a change. Have you always wanted to travel?"

"I have. I think I caught it from my mother. Her family were wealthy, but her brothers were the ones who got the education and went off travelling, while she was expected to stay home with her parents in Virginia. She couldn't go to college but she could read books about places she'd like to see. Her parents wanted her to find some quiet respectable young man and settle down, but when she met Pa, she wouldn't hear of it. Packed a suitcase, got married and went off to Texas with him. Told me to do the same thing! Pack my bags and travel I mean. Not get married."

"What does your father do?"

"He started out as a toolpusher – that's the head of a crew of oil men, but self-educated himself in geology. Eventually he struck off on his own and got lucky. Has three rigs. Now he occasionally gets contracts from different oil companies to prospect for oil. He's used the money coming in from that to buy a cattle ranch. I think he likes the excitement of looking for oil, but also enjoys staying at home and tending his cattle."

"Really? Cattle? On the farm back home, we have over fifty cattle! Not my favourite sort of thing though."

Karolina thought for a moment and decided that now was not the time to explain that her father had more than two thousand acres and a thousand head of cattle. Changing the subject she said, "Anyway, I wanted to tell you. I found out something interesting tonight about one of our suspects!"

"Well done! What is it?"

"Well, when we came through the customs shed, Sir Alfred was shouting at the customs officer."

"Yes, I saw that too"

"Well, what it sounded like was that the customs officer thought that Sir Alfred was bringing paintings into the country to sell. He said that Sir Alfred should have applied for approval and filled out documents and would have to pay a fine, or duty, or something! Sir Alfred was really mad and shouted that the pictures were his personal possessions that had been in his family for hundreds of years. But if so, why was he bringing them to Crete? He told the customs officer they were to decorate his house here, but he had told me that he was staying in a hotel, the best one of course, in Heraklion and he was going there to do business. He said he was going to have money to burn after he concluded his business and there would be a grand party!"

Alex suspected that Sir Alfred had said more than that and that he was probably still trying to persuade Karolina to be his special guest at the party, but he decided to say nothing. "So, you think Sir Alfred is selling off his family heirlooms, probably because he's short of money? Yesterday you mentioned something about an American millionaire on a yacht in Heraklion. You think he's the buyer?"

"Yes! I remember hearing that at least one American, a millionaire newspaper mogul, was touring the Mediterranean at the moment. He's buying up art for his collection. I'm sure Sir Alfred is going to sell those paintings to him because he's short of money. Which would make Sir Alfred a good suspect for searching Constantine's room for money or valuables and also for his murder!"

Alex was thoughtful for a few minutes. "We don't know for sure that Constantine was murdered."

"We don't? I thought you had decided he was!"

"I think he was, but I can't be absolutely sure. The evidence is circumstantial, but it's the most likely explanation that fits all the evidence."

"Well I think he was murdered and I think it was that jerk Sir Alfred who did it. Probably because he couldn't find what he wanted to steal, so he tried to beat it out of Constantine!"

"You don't like Sir Alfred then?" said Alex with a smile.

"Hmm. Whatever gave you that impression?" but before she could go into greater detail on Sir Alfred's sterling qualities, or lack thereof, the owner of the hotel came into the lounge. He wore a permanent broad smile across his face. As he came to the table, he introduced himself as Stephanos and asked what he could do for them.

Alex looked at Karolina and asked, "What would you like to drink?"

"Well there's no point in travelling, unless you try new experiences, is there? What do the locals drink?"

"That would probably be raki," said Alex uncertainly, "but that is a little strong."

"Oh no milady!" said Stephanos. "Raki is not a drink for young ladies. It is very nasty. Very nasty indeed. I have nice sherry for ladies. Is much nicer!"

"Raki really is very strong," explained Alex

"I was drinking bourbon when I was thirteen!" exclaimed Karolina, but decided not to add that it had tasted horrible and had made her sick. "I'm sure I can handle a little local hooch!" She noticed that Stephanos's daughter's head was peeking around the lounge door and that she was trying to stifle her laughter at her father.

Alex looked at Stephanos and shrugged his shoulders. "Maybe two glasses, a carafe of water and a small bottle of raki please Stephanos?" he said diplomatically.

Stephanos was obviously unhappy and felt that he knew better than they did that raki was not a nice drink for such a nice refined couple. Reluctantly he turned round and seeing his daughter laughing at the scene, he shooed her out before following her from the lounge.

"On a slightly different topic, have you heard that Captain Meunier has asked me to escort Constantine's belongings to Knossos and present them and his condolences to the granddaughter?"

"Yes, I heard that" said Karolina without expression. She was fine with Alex accompanying her and the other travellers for another day. She was finding that her initial impression of him may have been wrong and he wasn't quite the self-entitled, aristocratic idiot that she had first thought. Actually, now she thought about it, she quite liked his company, but she didn't want to give the misleading impression that she was encouraging any familiarity.

"What I found interesting was that also included in Constantine's belongings was that trunk, that was in the ship's cargo hold," said Alex.

"And you think that explains why our suspect searched Constantine's cabin twice? Because he couldn't find what he was looking for, as it was in the trunk? And that might also explain why he resorted to violence to get Constantine to tell him where whatever he was looking for was hidden?"

"Agreed. It's certainly a possibility. I just wish that Captain Meunier had not delivered the trunk and everything else to me, in front of all the other passengers."

"You think our suspect now knows where the money, or valuables, or whatever they are were hidden and more importantly, where they are now? You think they may make another attempt to steal whatever it is before we get to Knossos?"

"I do. I'm going to make sure I keep my eyes on that trunk until I hand it over to the granddaughter."

"I'll help too." said Karolina "I can keep watch just as well as you can."

"My dilemma now is, do I open the trunk and search it myself, or is that just not the done thing?"

They were interrupted by Stephanos bringing a tray of drinks to their table. He placed the tray down on the table and removed two small glasses and put one down in front of each Alex and Karolina. Then he very purposely picked up an unlabelled glass bottle from the tray and put it firmly and deliberately down in front of Alex. Then just as deliberately, he placed the water carafe in front of Karolina.

"Thank you Stephanos." said Alex and waited patiently for him to leave the lounge. Once they were alone again, he removed the rubber-washered stopper from the clear glass bottle and poured a small measure of the clear liquid into each of their glasses.

Alex knew what to expect from the raki. The navy had acclimatised him to the taste of a tot of real Pusser's navy rum and he knew to expect something similar from the raki. He raised his glass and looked curiously at Karolina.

Karolina was beginning to wonder at the wisdom of experimenting with what was obviously a strong liquor but was determined not to look like a lightweight in front of Alex. Picking up her glass she said confidently, "Salud!" and knocked the shot back in one.

Her eyes widened as the heat spread down her throat! "Oh! Goddam that's strong!"

Alex raised his glass to her in respect and knocked his own glass back.

Karolina tapped her empty glass on the table, indicating for Alex to refill it. "I think we should search the trunk. We can better protect any valuables if we know what and where they are. More importantly, there may be a clue as to who murdered Constantine."

Alex considered the points she'd made. "Agreed. Can't let politeness get in the way of catching a murderer. The trunk is in my room. I'll go up now and search it."

"I'm coming too."

"You can't come!"

"Oh yes I damn well can!" exclaimed Karolina. "You'll never do it properly!"

"What do you mean, I'll not do it properly?" he protested then realised he was being distracted from the real problem, "You can't come to my hotel bedroom! It's just not done!"

Karolina gave him a wicked smile, "Are you worried about your reputation?"

"No. Of course not. I'm thinking about yours."

"Well don't. If anyone needs to worry about my reputation it will be me and only me. Besides, we're the last ones about and if you don't tell, I won't tell. Drink up and get your butt moving."

Yet again Alex found himself at a loss for a response. Karolina just didn't behave the way that he had been brought up to expect young ladies to behave. She knew her own mind and was determined not to be controlled by anyone or anything. Realising that while he had been thinking, Karolina had knocked back her second drink and was looking at him impatiently. He hastily knocked back his own drink and struggled to his feet.

Without waiting for him, she got up from the table and as she marched out of the lounge, she threw back over her shoulder, "You're going to have to cut back on the drink if it slows you down like this,"

Alex caught up with her almost immediately because she stopped as soon as she entered the reception area. "Just out of academic interest," she said, looking around uncertainly, "where is your room anyway?"

Exasperated, Alex slipped past her, to lead her down the corridor next to the reception desk.

They reached Alex's room and entered. Alex carefully checked the tie that he'd draped over the trunk. It still crossed the lid of the trunk in exactly the same position where he'd left it. "Good," he said. "Nobody has disturbed the trunk."

Stepping up to the trunk, Karolina tried to lift the lid but it didn't budge. "It's locked," she said.

"No problem." Alex moved to the wardrobe and took out a wire coat hanger. Bending it backwards and forwards rapidly, he broke it into two pieces. He inserted each piece in turn into the gap between the wardrobe door and its frame, then closing the door on the wire, used the door as a vice to hold the end of the wire. Carefully he then bent the ends of each piece of wire until he was happy with the shapes he had created. Taking the wires in each hand he knelt in front of the trunk. Karolina watched with great interest as he manipulated the wires until satisfied, then he lent back and proudly lifted the lid of the now unlocked trunk.

Using a voice that could have come straight from an English duchess, Karolina said, "I think Mr. Armstrong, that if anyone's reputation has been damaged this evening, then it is yours!"

"Ah yes," said Alex, "When I was a boy in boarding school, we had tuck boxes similar to this. Picking the locks to retrieve your things the other boys had stolen was sort of a survival thing, you know."

"I think I understand, with the exception of what on earth is a tuck box?"

"Oh yes. Well, parents would send treats to their children during term time. Cakes and things. We'd call that 'tuck'. So, your tuck box is your trunk, where you hid it away with your other personal stuff, until you brought it out in the middle of the night to have a tuck party!"

Karolina was beginning to realise that it wasn't just the language that separated her from Alex, but a whole set of experiences that she had to struggle to understand.

While Alex had been talking, he had carefully been lifting out the contents of the trunk and laying them out on his bed. The top layer of contents had rested on a sturdy tray like structure that fitted closely into the trunk. Almost all of the contents were obviously Doctor Papadopoulos's clothes. The exceptions were a photo album, a beautiful white lace bridal veil and a black leather box, closed with a brass latch. Alex held the box up and a smile slowly spread across his face.

Impatiently, Karolina quickly took the box from Alex's hands and unclipped the latch. Lifting the lid, disappointment crossed her face. "Medical instruments," she said, showing the contents to Alex.

Alex carefully took each instrument from the box and studied them, before replacing them. "Yes, they're exactly what they look like. No precious metals. No gem stones," he said with the same note of disappointment as Karolina.

Meanwhile, Karolina had moved back to study the trunk. She was carefully feeling around inside and out and tapping on all the sides, top and base. "Nothing here either. No hidden catches, or secret compartments. She sat down on the edge of the bed next to Alex, not noticing how uncomfortable it made Alex. "This is not how it should work," she said. "In a Sherlock Holmes story we would have discovered a fabulous ruby gemstone in a hidden compartment."

Alex was re-examining the medical instruments. "I know, I was sure this would explain the mystery. Are you sure you haven't missed anything?"

Karolina turned and stared at Alex without saying a word.

After a few seconds, Alex realised what he had done. "Oh. Sorry! No of course you haven't."

Karolina looked at the neat piles of the contents of the trunk, laid out on the bed. "Looks like we need to come up with another idea for where his valuables could be hidden," she said, carefully beginning to repack the trunk. "Of course, our suspect may have already found what he was looking for." She looked sadly up at Alex, still sat on the bed."

"We can set a trap," he replied. "Find out if he's still looking for it." Taking out a small notebook he tore the edge of one of the sheets. Karolina had finished packing the trunk and was watching him closely. Carefully he placed the strip of paper on the top edge of the side of the trunk, with the tiniest amount projecting outward over the edge. Pressing this edge against the side of the trunk with his thumb, he slowly lowered the lid, leaving most of the strip inside, pinned between the lid and the side of the trunk. Removing his thumb slowly he said, "Now, if anyone opens the lid, the paper will fall inside and we'll know that it has been searched." He snapped the two latches closed, but deliberately did not re-lock it.

"Another skill learnt at your boarding school?"

"Absolutely," he replied. "I learnt loads of useful stuff there, just not much Latin vocab or English grammar!"

Karolina smiled and opened the door to his room. Stepping into the corridor she said, "See you for breakfast in the morning. Then in a deliberately louder more sensuous voice she called, "Goodnight darling," and blew him a kiss, closing the door on his suddenly embarrassed expression.

Chapter 17

Next morning Karolina came down to breakfast early. As she entered the reception area, the teenage girl that she had met last night came to her with a big smile across her face. Taking Karolina's elbow, she led her into the breakfast room and to the table of a quite jolly-looking young man with very little hair. He looked up at the two of them with a puzzled expression. The teenage girl turned to Karolina with a smile and said, "This man come to see Mr. Alex." Then she turned away, leaving Karolina standing in front of the stranger's table.

"I'm so sorry," he said, "I'm afraid the Greeks don't quite get the English necessity for introductions. My name's Charlie Armstrong. Very pleased to meet you . . . "

"Karolina McAllister. I'm still a little puzzled why the girl should think we were together?"

"Oh well, don't worry about that. We're very relaxed on Crete. Sit wherever you like, but you're very welcome to share my table . . ."

Deciding that informal was second nature to her, Karolina took a seat opposite the young man. "I'm guessing that you're Alex's cousin?"

"Spot on." said Charlie "You win a goldfish!"

Deciding that Charlie was either quite mad, or maybe the English as a whole were prone to moments of madness, Karolina said, "Goldfish?"

"Oh yes, my dear!" laughed Charlie. "Old tradition. Country fairs. Throw a wooden ball. Hit a coconut. Knock it down and win a prize

– goldfish or some such thing. Sorry. Didn't catch the accent till just now. Must be difficult adapting to our funny ways, eh?"

"We can certainly agree on that!" said Karolina.

"Got a telegram from Alex. He cancelled his plan to stay with us for last night. Can't say I blame him." said Charlie, as he sat there quietly appreciating the attractive young lady in front of him. "Wife's mother and sister staying with us. Kids in a perpetual state of riot! Even the dogs are looking for somewhere quiet to hide."

"I'm sure that's not the real reason he stayed here. I believe he was asked to make a diversion to Knossos."

"Oh yes – he put that in the telegram too. Awful business! And he doesn't really mind the kids anyway. Usually ends up being used as their climbing frame! They haven't seen him for a long time. But seeing as it's going to be a day or two before he's back, thought I'd come and surprise him. Get a second breakfast too, mind you!"

Karolina thought unkindly that by the look of his waistline, he could do with one less breakfast rather than one more breakfast, but decided to keep that to herself.

"So how long is it since you last saw Alex?"

"More than three years, 1915. He recovered here after the Dardanelles. He was pretty badly knocked about."

"Was that where he hurt his leg?"

"No. That was 1916. Battle of Jutland." Charlie paused, considering how much was private and how much he could tell this attractive young girl.

"What was the battle of Jutland?"

"Oh, you don't know? Big thing for the British. Our North Sea fleet went up against the German fleet. Lots of battleships. We didn't do so well. Lots of ships sunk. Lost three battleships, each with more than a thousand men and boys on board. Only a dozen or so men survived their sinking. Ships just blew to pieces! Alex's father was on one of them. HMS Indefatigable. We think Alex saw it happen."

Charlie was sombre for a moment, his eyes downcast, his imagination taking him far away.

Karolina quietly interrupted his thoughts. "What happened to Alex?"

"His ship, HMS Southampton, was one of the first to make contact with the German fleet. It was in the middle of the night. Took a terrible pounding. Had all her midship gun crews and most of her searchlight parties wiped out. She was blazing like a beacon with the cordite fires. Perfect target. Germans kept pounding away. Crew probably thought she'd blow up too. Alex was working on damage control, trying to get the guns back in operation, when a 4-inch shell hit. Blew superstructure down on top of him. Trapped under the wreckage, don't you know. In and out of consciousness. Well, there were fires all around him. Dead and wounded too. Fires lit up the whole ship. No way to put the fires out, while still trying to fight the Germans. Wasn't until a long time later that night that a couple of stokers heard his cries. Lifted the wreckage off him. He was in a bad way. He'd lost a lot of blood. Leg was smashed. Thought it would be amputated. Suffered for months after. But he still insists he was one of the lucky ones though."

Karolina was appalled. She simply stared at Charlie. "Oh God." she said. "I just remembered; I accused him of having had an easy war, sitting it out in London!"

Charlie looked at her and shook his head. "Damned if I want to see what you'd call a hard war then."

Karolina felt almost sick.

Conversation pretty much stalled for a while. Karolina ordered coffee and toast and Charlie finished off his second breakfast of the day.

Alex came down to breakfast shortly after. It had taken a long time to get off to sleep, thinking about the events of the last few days, trying not to keep thinking about Karolina, but eventually he had sunk into a deep uninterrupted sleep. The best night's sleep since leaving Brindisi and he had to admit to himself he was now looking forward to the trip to Knossos. On seeing Charlie seated with Karolina at the breakfast table, he'd let out a happy shout. Charlie had jumped up and with a big smile on his face, he spent the next few minutes laughing, hugging and pounding Alex on his back. Eventually, Alex pleaded for mercy and came and sat down next to Karolina.

"So you've met this old reprobate already have you?" laughed Alex.

"I have." said Karolina. He's been telling me terrible stories about what you got up to in boarding school!"

"Oh no!" exclaimed Alex. "Not the one about matron's laundry!"

"Alex, you have to watch this one. I never told her any stories about your school days. She's bluffing you!"

"I make no apologies," said Karolina. "It worked didn't it. And success is its own justification! So, what is this story about matron's laundry?"

"Another time maybe. You may have to ply me with raki again, if you want me to tell you that story!"

"Raki!" exclaimed Charlie with delight. "Don't tell me you two have been drinking raki already?"

"Drink it? She throws it back like water!"

Using the same English duchess voice she had used the night before, Karolina said "Mr. Armstrong, you do me a disservice. I merely sipped the aperitif, as any well brought up lady would do."

Alex lifted his hand to his face to shield his mouth from Karolina and in a stage whisper to Charlie said, "More like as any old chief petty officer would do."

Charlie looked at Karolina and smiled. "Looks to me like you've been taking good care of old Alex for me. He's not usually this happy you know. Thank you for that."

"Oh, he needs taking care of," replied Karolina. "Gets into all sort of trouble otherwise."

Alex sat back and crossed his arms. "Pots and kettles come to mind after that remark, Miss McAllister," he said.

"So anyway, I understand the two of you leave soon for Knossos via Rethymno?"

"Absolutely Charlie. But I have a feeling, from the absence of our fellow travellers at the breakfast table, that we may be late starting."

"Well that's fine by me. More time to chat. Let's get some more coffee and dredge up some really embarrassing stories from Alex's childhood."

"Yes." said Karolina, "Remind me. Where were we up to with 'the mystery of matron's laundry' . . . ?"

Chapter 18

Alex proved to be correct about the late start. Their transport arrived about fifteen minutes late, but most of the passengers were still coming down for breakfast. Alex was amused to recognise the vehicle as an old Crossley 34cwt truck, probably a military ambulance or some such from the Great War, that had been converted into what he would have called a charabanc. It seated twelve people in four rows of three, with an overhanging shelf at the rear for luggage. The last row of seats had also been removed to provide even more luggage space. The remaining seats had cushions covered in a thick tough woven material like carpet. The effect was much like sitting on a church hassock. A canvas roof gave notional shelter from rain or sun. The modifications had been completed with several shiny new coats of paint, so that the vehicle looked quite festive in red, green and yellow. From the way Stephanos greeted the driver, it appeared he was a good friend or close family relative to Stephanos.

Alex made sure that Constantine's luggage was safely loaded and threw up his own overnight bag before climbing up onto the front seat. The rest of his luggage was in Charlie's safe hands until he came back from Knossos. Charlie waved up at Alex in the omnibus, then left him to return to his family, promising to unleash what he called his demon horde of children on Alex on his return.

Soon after that, Karolina came out of the hotel. She was dressed in a long, dropped waist, navy blue top with a square neck, embroidered with white and red beadwork. She'd matched this with a white, knee length, cotton skirt and her wide-brimmed cloche hat. The effect was stunning.

Seeing the young teenage girl from the hotel, Karolina immediately smiled and went over to talk to her and gave her what Alex suspected was a generous tip, together with a parting hug and a kiss on the cheek. At first the girl seemed to refuse to take the tip, then threw her arms round Karolina's neck, before rushing off. Karolina then jumped up into the omnibus.

More time was wasted as luggage was loaded, unloaded, repacked and loaded again. Passengers boarded, then disembarked and re-boarded, after retrieving items from their luggage that they felt would be absolutely essential on the trip, or recovering items from their rooms that had just remembered that they had left behind.

Alex and Lord Thomas shared the front bench seat with the driver. Alex was pleased to see Sir Alfred fail in his attempt to sit next to Karolina. She ended up sharing the middle bench seat with Mr. and Mrs. Webster. Sir Alfred was disgruntled to find himself relegated to the last unoccupied seat on the rear bench with Dai and Vasiliki. Once all the passengers were seated, the driver went to the front of the vehicle and inserted the crank handle. Swinging the handle more and more aggressively, eventually the engine reluctantly stirred into noisy life and it looked like the travellers were finally on their way. Just as the vehicle began to move, the teenage girl re-appeared and ran up to the vehicle. Reaching up, she thrust a beautiful blue scarf into Karolina's hands. Backing away, she smiled happily and waved vigorously as the brightly painted vehicle slowly rolled away down the narrow street.

Chapter 19

The road ran East out of Chania toward Rethymno and then onward to Knossos and Heraklion, more or less along the North coast of Crete. Initially it was through narrow, cobbled streets, with houses and shops crowding in on both sides. The houses were small and mostly covered in stucco, with their colourfully painted wooden shutters thrown back to let in air. The occasional grander house, constructed from brick, rose above the smaller buildings, some set back slightly from the road, protected by ornate wrought iron railings. Many of the houses were decorated with colourful plants in pots. The shops were stocked with brightly coloured goods hanging from hooks, or with boxes of produce stacked in front of them. As the omnibus passed through the streets, children would jump up onto the running board and catch a ride. They would laugh and hold out a hand hoping for some small change. Even if refused, the children would continue to hang on, happy just to practice their few words of English with the strangers.

Karolina sat back, enjoying the experience, watching everything as they passed along the road, soaking up the beauty. Quite quickly they emerged from the more heavily populated area of the town and the cobbled streets gave way to a gravel and stone trackway. The houses and shops fell behind them and were replaced by fields interspersed with widely spread-out farm huts and villas.

The sun beat down on them and Karolina was glad of the protection from the lightweight canvas roof of the omnibus. Soon, as the omnibus crawled out of the relatively flat land around Chania, the road began to wind up into the pine clad Cretan hills, Mrs. Webster turned to Karolina and began a conversation.

"I'm surprised your parents allowed you to make this trip on your own. I think it's very daring!"

"Well, I grew up in Texas and they teach you to take care of yourself there. Pa taught me to ride when I was five, shoot when I was eight. I could rope a young steer by the time I was ten."

"Didn't your mother object to your father bringing you up as such a tom boy?"

"Not at all. She knew I enjoyed it and wouldn't ever get in my way of doing what I wanted. But she also taught me responsibility and the need to accept the consequences of my choices. And she encouraged me to learn by reading and how to behave in polite company." Karolina thought a little guiltily of how she had enjoyed embarrassing Alex outside his bedroom the night before, but decided not to mention anything about that little incident. "She also taught me about how our ranch was run, how to do the books and how to manage the ranch hands."

"But won't your husband do all that for you, after you marry?"

"I'm not sure I'll let him," replied Karolina, but her mind was elsewhere when she said it, thinking of her now dead fiancé. "My mother and Pa run the ranch jointly and enjoy doing it that way. They're 'equally yoked' as Pa always says. Seems to be a great way to live."

"Have your parents been to Europe?"

"No. Difficult to get Pa to take a break or to leave the ranch. I think he'd pine." Karolina smiled at the thought. "The furthest mother has been is to New York. She wanted to see the great museums there. When I was about fourteen, she took me and her sister with her. That's probably the first time I became interested in archaeology, seeing exhibitions from Egypt, Sumer, Phoenicia, Phrygia, Greece . . . so many of them. All so exotic. And of course, Crete. That's where I heard about Harriet Boyd Hawes from Boston who excavated sites in Crete. That's also when my mother told me of the story of the Minotaur and the labyrinth and I've been fascinated ever since. It's an opportunity of a life-time to see the palace of Knossos."

"Do you not have any brothers or sisters then?"

"No, just me. Pa says I'm trouble enough." She smiled. "Says I put them off the thought of any more kids."

"I'm sure you didn't. We'd love to have more children, but I'm afraid it's too late for us."

"You said more children. How many children do you have?"

"None, dear. We had one child, a daughter – Marjorie - but she died when very young from tetanus."

"I'm so sorry Mrs. Webster."

"I imagine she would be very similar to you dear, if she had had the chance to grow up." Mrs. Webster looked at Karolina and then dabbed a tear from her eyes. "Grief is so hard to bear and it's a terrible unnatural thing when a child dies before it's parents."

"You have my sympathy. I can understand your sadness Mrs. Webster and of course for your husband too."

"Mr. Webster was terribly angry as well as sad. He loved Marjorie so much and he felt he should have protected her. She was truly the apple of his eye and she should never have had to die, not so young."

Murder on Crete

Together Karolina and Mrs. Webster fell silent, each lost in their own thoughts, as they watched the beautiful, majestic countryside unroll.

As the converted military truck bumped and jerked along the road into the hills, Alex glanced back over his shoulder. He saw Dai and Vasiliki, on the rear most bench seat, chatting away. He was amused to note Sir Alfred's disgusted expression as he sat next to them, as the dust from the roadway swirled up from the front wheels and settled on the rearmost passengers in a fine layer of orange dust.

After nearly an hour of driving, they emerged onto a high coast road with dusty, desolate hills, sloping steeply up to their right, but a beautiful view of the blue Mediterranean Sea down to their left. Further away across the sea Alex could see hills on a headland on other side of the bay. Beneath them, plying its way out of the bay he could see a small ferry boat. The road curled and twisted along the side of the hill for miles, often with sheer drops a few feet from the crumbling edges of the road. Gaps in the trees on the left of the road gave them many views of the Mediterranean below them. Eventually they reached Kalyves and, turning away from the sea, they climbed towards the mountains, cutting across the headland. The narrow winding roads took them higher into the hills, passing through small hamlets and villages, often consisting of just a few houses. Tumbled piles of rocks indicated the sites of small rock slides, that caused the truck to crawl slowly past. The sun had now risen high to their right into the cloudless sky. Caves could be seen in the hills overlooking the road and small churches were also common, together with many small shrines.

Karolina tapped Alex on the shoulder and pointed to a particularly colourful shrine as they passed it. "I've been looking at all these roadside shrines," she said. "Seeing how dangerous these roads are, I can image a lot of deaths, but so many? Does each shrine mean that someone died there?"

"Not necessarily," said Alex, leaning back. "The locals also put shrines up as a way of saying thanks, where perhaps someone had a near miss, but survived."

Karolina nodded. One of the things that had helped her through her dark spells, was constantly reminding herself of what she still had and being grateful for it. She decided that each shrine she saw from now on, would not be a signpost of grief, but she would assume it to be a signpost of gratitude.

Sometime later, conversation amongst the passengers had died out, but Karolina was still enjoying the spectacular scenery as much as ever. Karolina saw an abbey or maybe a monastery standing high up on the mountain to her left and then the road began to wind downwards through sharp turns and hairpins following the course of a river through a wide, rocky valley, towards the sea. Goats and sheep grazed alongside the road under the shade of olive trees. After what felt like an eternity of being bumped and jostled, they eventually reached the mouth of the river where it met the sea and crossed over on a rickety wooden bridge. Karolina gasped at the sight of a small fairy-tale white church, seeming to be floating on top of the sea a hundred yards from land. As she watched the church getting closer, she realised it actually sat on a low foundation of rocks and was linked to the mainland by a long low causeway of stones.

Shortly after they left the river and the floating church behind, the driver pulled the omnibus over in front of a building that seemed to be a combination roadside taverna, coffee house and vegetable shop. The driver indicated by waving his arms that the travellers should disembark, then disappeared into the taverna, coming out shortly afterwards with a white enamel bucket of water and a suspicious looking clear glass bottle filled with a colourless liquid. The driver took a small swig from the glass bottle and started to dribble water from the bucket over the vehicle's radiator. Clouds of steam rose up as the radiator began to cool. Looking across to Alex, Karolina raised her eyebrows in a question. "What do you think the driver has in that bottle?"

"I'm sure it's just a bottle of water," he said, but without much conviction.

Shaking her head, Karolina followed Mrs. Webster into the taverna come coffee house.

Alex followed them both in and bought himself a coffee and a couple of pastries before going back outside. Seeing Lord Thomas sat at a roadside table under the shade of an olive tree, Alex walked over and asked if it was okay to join him.

"Of course, my boy. Take the weight off and sit!"

"How are you holding up, sir?"

"Fine my boy. Been through worse. Lap of comfort and luxury compared to France. If I ignore the shaking and bumping in a way it's quite restful. And this sunshine is wonderful!"

"Good," said Alex, "I was wondering if you'd had a chance to talk to any more of our fellow travellers?"

"I did as a matter of fact. Had a chat with that Welshman, Dai. I agree with your impression of him. Definitely black market and also those Egyptian artefacts are probably illegal and being smuggled back into Britain. He had the cheek to pump me for names of chaps who might be interested in buying some!"

Alex smiled. "What about the Greek, Vasiliki? Have you been talking to him too?"

"Yes. I had a chat over breakfast with him. He's not very talkative mind you. I noticed him first when he came aboard at Corfu, so I asked if he lived there and he confirmed that he did. Said he works in a cassino there. He dropped a few names, trying to impress me and he mentioned Prince George, just like our poor doctor did."

Alex took this all in and thought about it. "Talking of the doctor," he pulled out Doctor Constantine's business card and showed it to Lord Thomas, "Have you come across this company before? It's a medical laboratory."

"My God!" exclaimed Lord Thomas, the colour rushing to his face. "Damn and blast the man to hell and back!"

Alex was amazed at the reaction he had produced. He watched the man closely as he struggled to contain his anger.

"Yes, I have heard of that company. It's infamous." He took a few more deep breaths to regain his composure and continued, struggling to keep his voice calm, "Years back before the war there was a huge scandal. This laboratory was producing the anti-toxin for use against diphtheria. I don't know if you know how they do it, but they harvest blood that contains the antibodies from a horse. A horse can produce gallons of the blood if you spread the collections over a long time. They sold the anti-toxin and it was used widely on children. But the damn company was cutting all sorts of corners. They didn't test the blood before they sold the serum. Didn't find out until too late that the horse had contracted tetanus. The anti-toxin was given to children all over Greece and many of them died of tetanus because of it. Turned out that the company had friends in high places and got away with just a slap on the wrist. Now I know that Doctor Constantine was the owner of the laboratory I don't feel at all bad about him falling overboard."

Alex sat and digested the new information. It seemed that they may have missed another motive for the murder of Doctor Constantine Papadopoulos.

It took the other travellers nearly an hour to satisfy their needs for a break and refreshment, despite much heckling along from the driver. Eventually he got them all back on the omnibus and he repeated the performance of starting the engine with the hand crank. This time the process appeared to require muttered curses from the driver as well as a more vigorous cranking. Eventually, the engine reluctantly grumbled into life and they set off, still heading East along the coastal road, which would now take them almost all the way to Rethymno.

Again, Karolina marvelled at the marvellous views as the truck trundled and bounced along. The rocky barren mountains were now being replaced by dark green, pine clad mountains, with the sun hanging high over them in the cloudless blue sky. After a further hour she reached forward to tap Alex on the shoulder again, "How much longer do you think?"

Murder on Crete

Alex shrugged his shoulders and leant across to the driver to ask. The driver took both hands off the wheel and started gesticulating wildly to Alex, speaking a mixture of English and Greek. "From what I can make out we're probably still an hour from Rethymno. So it might be mid-afternoon before we reach it. Much later than scheduled. I think the driver said this is due to English travellers having no sense of crones – or thinking about it, he may actually have said 'chronos'. No sense of time. Difficult to say really. There was a lot of head slapping and arm waving. I didn't like to ask too many questions when he didn't have his hands on the steering wheel."

Karolina sat back on her bench seat and sighed. She decided that travelling with the English could be very frustrating, but never boring.

The road wound onwards and the afternoon became still warmer. Eventually the road crossed first one then a second steep ravine on narrow rickety wooden bridges. The ravines were rocky and sheer-sided, running down from the mountains on their right into the sea on the left. The road was now some distance away from and high above the coast. All of the passengers perked up and took interest when they noticed, down below them on the coast, a huge coastal fortress sitting atop a hill. Sheer walls rose up to enclose a hill covered in dark green leafy trees, with the golden dome of a mosque rising from the centre of the trees. As they got closer, they saw that the fortress overlooked an ancient harbour, with streets and buildings crammed within the town walls. Outside the walls of the town was a Greek orthodox church, a cemetery and a large public garden with tall palm and pine trees. Surrounding all of this were fields and olive trees and many small houses.

The truck drove along the narrow winding roads on the side of the hill and the driver turned back to look at the passengers and shouted "Rethymno!"

They pulled up in front of a beautiful white stucco three-storey hotel on their right, looking down over the town, half a mile away on their left. The hotel had balconies looking out towards the sea and the town, decorated with masses of colourful plants. The driver ushered his passengers off the vehicle and up the dozen or so steps towards the front door. He used both his hands to make gestures of eating with a knife and fork. As they moved into the hotel Alex casually held back from the others and paused on the front porch admiring the view down the hill to the town. When all the other travellers were inside, he walked back to the rear of the omnibus and checked Constantine's luggage. The small white paper tag was still visible wedged underneath the lid of trunk. Satisfied, he turned and followed the rest of the passengers into the hotel just as the driver emerged carrying his now familiar white enamel bucket and his clear glass bottle.

Between slow service and travellers who took their time indulging in fine wine and good food, the belated lunch stretched out to more than an hour. Eventually the travellers began to wander back outside and the driver, who had been snoring loudly on a long bench at the side of the hotel, made his way back to the omnibus. His arrival back at the bus was marked by a loud shout and a stream of Greek. If his exclamations didn't contain swear words, they must have contained many appeals to the gods, along the lines of 'Why me oh Lord!'. Reaching a peak in his outburst, the driver lashed out a kick at one of the vehicle's front tyres.

Alex approached him cautiously, as the other passengers looked on. He quickly spotted that the driver's gesticulations and most of his excited vocabulary was directed at a pool of water that had formed under the front of the vehicle. The radiator had never had a grill protecting it, so the front of the copper mesh was exposed directly to view. He saw a small gash in the copper mesh almost at the base of the radiator. Looking closely at the hole, he saw a slow drip of water emerge - explaining the driver's emotional behaviour and frustration.

Several minutes passed with discussions between passengers, the hotel owner and the driver, before it was established beyond doubt that the omnibus would not be going any further today and that to the great pleasure of the owner, there were sufficient, most beautiful and luxurious rooms in his most beautiful and luxurious hotel and he could accommodate all of the passengers comfortably. The owner called for more staff from the hotel and the luggage was unloaded and piled under the overhanging veranda at the front of the hotel. Guests signed the register and were escorted to their rooms, before the staff returned to the pile of luggage and began to deliver it back to the relevant owners.

Alex waited in the lounge area at the bottom of the stairs for Karolina to return from her room and then indicated with a nod for her to follow him outside.

"What is it?" she asked.

"How would you like a leisurely walk down to the harbour and a little chat?" he asked.

"That sounds like a perfect way to brighten up my day. Which way do you suggest?"

Picking the narrow lane that zig-zagged downhill from the hotel towards the town, Alex said, "Let's try this way."

Together, they casually strolled off down the lane and soon reached the outskirts of the town. As they approached the town, they entered into and walked through a municipal garden, taking advantage of the shade from its palm and pine trees. To the right of the municipal garden, they passed a cemetery and an open market place. Reluctantly leaving the shade of the garden, they passed through an ancient arched gateway set in the town walls, into the narrow bustling streets of Rethymno. On either side of the street, small shops and businesses stood shoulder to shoulder with each other. Most of the shops comprised of a single arched front, with inclined columns either side of the arch, sloping gently back into the buildings structure. High flagged pavements ran along either side of the cobbled streets. As Alex and Karolina passed through the streets, the shopkeepers happily called out, offering their goods to the young couple. The range of goods on offer was impressive, from leather belts, shoes and boots to wine, sponges, herbs, spices and food of all sorts, together with colourful linens, lace and pottery.

As they strolled through the streets, they found it easier to step down from the high granite kerbstones and walk in the road, weaving between the people, donkeys, goats and sheep that crowded the byways. Many of the passers-by were wearing local costume. The women wore white baggy blouses, often decorated with lace at the neck and cuffs, with embroidered coloured jackets or waistcoats and dark ankle-length full skirts. Reds and blues abounded. Men typically wore the traditional full-cut baggy trousers, or 'vraka', tucked into tall boots, with white shirts and sleeveless waistcoats or sashes.

Other narrow streets and alleys crossed and branched off from their street as they walked along, until eventually it opened out into a small square. The square was filled with tables and chairs belonging to a taverna. Overhead vines with purple flowers criss-crossed the square, giving shade to the taverna's patrons. Alex and Karolina found the idea of coffee and a bite to eat too tempting to refuse and took a small table. A short Greek man with curly silver hair and a welcoming smile, came bustling out of the café. He introduced himself as Stamatis Galeros, the owner, and asked what they would like.

"I think I'd like a coffee and something to snack on. What do you have?" asked Karolina.

"I will bring you my meze! You will like it very much, I'm sure. And for you sir? The same?"

"Absolutely. That will suit me too."

As Stamatis left to bring their order, they sat and watched the people passing by. Alex admired the ancient columned stone wall at one end of the square. The wall had three small fountains bubbling water into troughs, set within three small niches. Alex pointed to the fountains and different carvings on the wall and suggested, "Roman?"

Karolina studied it a little longer and pronounced, "Probably Venetian."

Alex nodded knowledgeably.

Eventually, Stamatis returned with the coffee and a host of small plates. As Alex and Katrina both exclaimed at the size of the wonderful selection, Stamatis happily sat down with them and named and described each dish to them.

"These are pita bread, these are asparagus. Here is feta cheese. Here is fava bean dip and humus, Tzatziki and red pepper dip. Here are other local vegetables, local olives and figs."

Karolina asked, "What are these small pasty-like items?"

"Ah. Those are 'Tiropitakia' which are small cheese pies and this is the 'meli' or honey as you call it, to pour over the Tiropitakia."

"I say! Those are really good!" exclaimed Alex, having tried one already.

"Well don't think that you're going to eat them all by yourself," said Karolina, quickly claiming one for herself with a smile.

"There is no problem, sirs and madams. I will bring more at once. I'm so very pleased you enjoy!" said Stamatis, rising happily from his chair and bustling back into the taverna.

For a few minutes they enjoyed comparing and sampling the dishes in front of them, but finally agreed that the favourite for both of them were the tiny cheese pies drizzled in honey.

After they had made a good attempt to demolish the array of dishes and refused Stamatis smiling offer to bring even more, Alex turned to Karolina, "I've found out something very significant about our Doctor Constantine."

"Oh really?" said Karolina. "Tell me more."

"Apparently, he wasn't such a nice old man as we thought. Apparently, his laboratory was involved in a scandal before the war, that resulted in several young children dying."

"Oh wow! Said Karolina, before pausing thoughtfully. "I don't suppose you know the details of how the children died?"

"I do. The laboratory was producing anti-toxin for use against diphtheria. The medicine became contaminated by the tetanus bacteria and when it was given to children, many died from the contamination."

"That's it!" exclaimed Karolina. "While they were living in Greece before the war started, Mr. and Mrs Webster had a young girl. She died of tetanus. Mrs. Webster said her husband was very angry about it and that it should never have been allowed to happen! Mr. Webster must have recognised Constantine, or found out about his involvement and finished him off!"

"We don't know that for sure," said Alex

"It sure fits well though!" said Karolina excitedly.

"They aren't the only ones with that motive. Lord Thomas was the one who told me about it and he was furious when I showed him the laboratory's name on Constantine's business card. He acted surprised and it did seem genuine, but he could have already known about the doctor's connection to the laboratory and decided to be judge, jury and executioner."

"Lord Thomas is a sweetie. It wasn't him. Mr. Webster is a much better bet."

They sat in silence for a while. Alex was the first to break the silence. "Agreed. But we need evidence before we can say anything. But there's something else. You know the water leak on the truck? I think it was sabotage. The copper edges of the hole were bright and shiny, with no sign of aging or corrosion. There was a gash about an inch long and the edges had been pushed in. Something was stabbed into the radiator. Something like one of the knives we were using to eat our lunch."

"Why would anyone do that?"

"Well, it could be Sir Alfred wants another go at getting you to come to his party?" suggested Alex.

"Ha! Chance would be a fine thing! Creepy jerk!"

"Who me? That's not a nice . . ."

"No, not you, you idiot. Sir Alfred. You're not a creep, just stupid!" she said, laughing.

"Well now we have my strengths of character sorted out . . . If it's not Sir Alfred up to his tricks, then I think it's the murderer. I think he was seeing Constantine's trunk drifting out of his reach if we get to Knossos tonight and decided to play for time. Bet you ten to one that when we get back, the trunk will have been searched!"

"No bet. But, if you're right, you have to pick up the tab for dinner tonight! It's the price you pay for being a know-it-all and an idiot!"

Chapter 20

Dinner that evening was a buffet. On the second floor of the hotel was a long room with floor to ceiling wooden French doors, looking out onto a balcony, with views down the hill to the old town and port of Rethymno. The after nightfall the view was simply spectacular, with the lights of the old town dancing in the evening air. Both the dining room and the balcony were laid out with small round tables for the dinners. The tables were covered in pristine white table clothes, each with a small red lamp in the middle. On the inner wall of the dining room a long, narrow rectangular table was covered with a variety of local dishes. A young schoolboy with masses of dark curly hair, dressed in a white waiter's uniform that was much too big for him, stood by the table eager to help. Alex and Karolina arrived at the same time. Alex smiled at her and whispered, "I checked the tell-tale on the trunk before coming down and it's been searched. Looks like I'm buying dinner."

Karolina nodded and whispered back, "That's very interesting. Now if we can just find out who searched the trunk, we'll get a goldfish!"

That stopped Alex in his tracks as he tried to make sense of her remark. Eventually he put it down to another crazy American expression and followed her to the buffet.

As they wondered down the buffet table, the young boy came up to them and offered to help.

"This is very good, sirs and madams," he said, pointing to a dish of halved eggplant, stuffed with tomatoes, onions and olives, with roasted feta cheese on top. "It is called 'Imam Bayildi'."

"I've never heard of it," said Alex, "What does that mean?"

"It means 'Help, the imam has fallen'," laughed the boy. "My mother says that during Ramadan, many, many years ago, an imam had not eaten all day. A Christian farmer's wife was cooking this dish and it smelt so good, that the imam leant so far out of his minaret to smell it better, that he fell out. And the people shouted . . . "

"Help, the imam has fallen!" laughed Karolina and Alex together.

"Well, I guess, I'd better try it then," said Karolina

"Me too," said Alex. "And can you also make a third plate of it for me?" After escorting Karolina, with their full plates, to a table, he went back to the boy and collected the extra plate of food. Taking this and a small carafe of wine, he left the room. Coming back a few minutes later, he saw Karolina's puzzled expression.

"Just before dinner, I went to check on our transport. The driver is working on it by lamp light, removing the radiator. He's going to take it into town in the morning and find a mechanic to repair it. He says we'll be back on the road by lunchtime tomorrow. I thought he deserved some food and drink."

Karolina looked at him sitting across from her and decided that he might be a know-it-all and an idiot, but he could also, just sometimes, be quite sweet as well. She noticed she had been staring at him in silence for several seconds and he was starting to look worried, so she decided to change the topic.

"So, our little trap, with Constantine's trunk worked?"

"It did. Whoever was searching for whatever it is, is still looking."

". . . and he sabotaged our old jalopy to give himself time to do that."

"I think so. We still have no proof though."

"Well, we still have until tomorrow to figure out another trap to catch him."

They both fell silent and resumed eating their dinners.

Karolina was the next to speak. "I did a little investigating of my own, after we got back from our walk into town."

"Oh yes?" said Alex with interest.

"Yes. Mr. and Mrs. Webster were sat out on the veranda, admiring the view. I joined them for a drink – no raki! Just white wine! But I thought I would see how Mr. Webster would react to mention of Constantine's name, so I talked about how sad it was for him to have fallen overboard and how his granddaughter was now all alone in the world."

" . . and?"

"He was sympathetic. He said he would be sure to give their condolences to her if he had chance to. He would also see if there was anything they could do to help her . . . "

"Do you think that was because he felt guilty?"

"I don't think so. Of course, he could just be a good actor and if he had thrown Constantine overboard, he would know to keep his feelings to himself, but it seemed genuine to me."

"Well, seems like as one door opens, another door closes then."

"Let's not rule him out completely, but I don't think he did it." said Karolina. "I'm not the best judge of character though. For instance, I thought you might be a nice guy, when I first met you," she laughed. She took another mouthful of her dinner, then stopped. "About that."

"Yes?"

"Well, when we first met, at dinner with Captain Meunier," she paused.

"Yes?"

"Well, . . . I was mean to you. I said you'd had an easy war in London. I didn't know about what you'd been through."

"And what exactly had I been through?" said Alex in a steely voice.

"You know. Jutland. That stuff." Oh god thought Karolina, if there was ever a way to screw up a friendship, she could sure find it! "I'm sorry," she said. "You don't want to talk about it I know, but I just wanted to apologise."

Alex said nothing.

After a long, tense silence, Alex blurted out "That Charlie is a blabbermouth and an ass!"

They continued to eat their meals in awkward silence.

When Karolina had finished, she said in a much softer voice than she had used before, "You know, the Temple of Knossos is quite spectacular, at least to an archaeologist it is. If you would like, when we get there, I could show you round, tell you all about the myths, the labyrinth, the minotaur . . .?" Worriedly, she watched Alex's face as he considered her offer.

Finally, he took a deep breath. "Thank you for your offer" he said.

Glancing around the room but without looking at her, he said "I'm sure that would interest some of our fellow travellers, but . . . "

"Great!" she said enthusiastically, before he could finish his sentence with a reason to turn down her invitation, "I like nothing better than to bore people about archaeology! And there's so much of it, I can bore for hours!"

He gave a quick smile, but his expression quickly became serious again and remained that way for the rest of the meal.

Chapter 21

Alex had another bad night, waking again from the same recurring nightmare of his terrible experience during the battle of Jutland. Worse was the knowledge that during his nightmare he had been struggling to shout for help and the suspicion that it probably meant he had been making enough noise to be heard by other guests in the hotel. He hoped that no one would be able to identify which room the cries had been coming from. His mind had been slow to stop reliving his nightmare, but eventually he had lain there trying to distract himself by concentrating on the problem of determining who was Constantine's murderer. He'd been lying in bed for some time before finally deciding that it was now a reasonable hour to get up.

Coming into the breakfast room, he was surprised to see he had been beaten there by Karolina, who was sat at an outside table sipping coffee and reading the book she had borrowed from Doctor Constantine.

On seeing Karolina out on the patio, he paused indecisively before going out through the French doors. He was about to take a table inside when Karolina looked up and saw him. She called out cheerily, "Well if it isn't my favourite limey!"

At the last second he changed his mind and walked out onto the patio to join her at her table. As he stood there he said, "Interesting thing about the word 'limey', it originated . . . "

Karolina completed the sentence for him ". . . from the practice of the British Navy to put lime in the rum ration of its sailors to prevent scurvy. They didn't know why it prevented scurvy, but it did." Then she had to laugh at the disappointed expression that crossed his face. "I'm sorry. I think I stole your thunder. Would you like to share my table and you can even the score by telling me some amusing fact that I don't know?" As Alex hesitated, she continued, "You know, just because your country has so much history, you shouldn't ever assume that you're the only one who knows anything about it!"

"I can promise you, not everyone is like you though. Just how did you get to know so much?"

"My Pa says I ask too many questions and, I'm also looking around and noticing things all the time." As she said that she was noticing how tired Alex was looking. However, she was determined to not repeat her mistake of last night. Even though the apology she had made then had been genuine, she realised that what he had heard when she had spoken, was pity. So, she bit her tongue and kept quiet – hard though that was for her.

The same young boy they had met the night before came out of the kitchen and stood by Karolina's table and smiled at the pair. Karolina said to Alex, "The croissants and pastries they serve are excellent if you'd like to try them?

"Okay," he said and turning to the boy he nodded, "Pastries and coffee please."

" . . . and more coffee for me too, please," she called out as the boy walked away. "Rather than standing there like that, wondering what to do, why don't you sit down? The boy is going to bring your order to my table anyway."

Alex hadn't realised that he'd been standing there undecided, but quickly pulled the other chair back and carefully sat down. He still felt awkward after last night and had started to worry whether or not he had been rude to Karolina. He decided to push on and act as if that part of their conversation about his leg had never happened.

"I've been thinking about our problem. We have no real evidence that proves anything for certain."

Karolina was interested to note that he was calling it 'our' problem now. She wasn't really sure why, but that made her feel better. "No, but we're pretty sure it was murder and we know who the suspects are," she said.

"But we still have no evidence we could take to the police."

"Okay, I'll give you that."

"Last night you described what we did with Constantine's trunk, as setting a trap."

"Yes. I remember,"

"Well, as I lay awake thinking about it, that kept coming back to me. What if we set another trap. One that would catch the murderer?"

"Keep talking. You have my undivided attention."

"Well, I need your help. Would you like to come for another walk into town with me, after breakfast, then I'll see if I can explain my idea to you?"

Karolina looked at him curiously, but she was prepared to wait and let him explain his plan in his own time, at least if he didn't take the devil's own time do it!

They met after breakfast, outside the hotel and followed the same path as before, down into the town. They entered the old town through the same ancient archway in the town walls and continued to explore the narrow streets. This time instead of following the main street, they decided to explore a different route through the town and turned left into a street that seemed to contain blacksmiths, cart builders and harness makers. They stopped to admire one shop with a wooden donkey saddle on display. As they walked on, Alex explained his idea.

"Our advantage is that the murderer is still searching for something in Constantine's luggage. We've also searched the luggage and not found anything, but the murderer doesn't know that. That's what I mean by saying we have the advantage."

"Go on."

"Can you help me buy something that looks like a jewel box? Doesn't have to be too expensive, in fact it should look a little old and worn. Then we can pretend . . . "

"Alex, I could kiss you!" said Karolina excitedly and Alex stepped back hastily. He might have got away without Karolina noticing his reaction, but he stepped back into a basket of harnesses and leather work on the road outside a shop. He tried to keep his balance, but his injured leg couldn't support him and he fell backwards onto the rest of the shopkeeper's goods. Lying on top of the baskets he looked up threateningly at Karolina, daring her to show sympathy. She looked at him wide eyed, holding her breath for a second, then she burst out laughing.

Together she and the shopkeeper reached down to help him up, Karolina still laughing happily. To Alex's embarrassment, he noticed her laughter was infectious and the shopkeeper and one or two passers-by began to smile at him as well.

"Well thank you for your concern for my dignity Miss McAllister," said Alex with mock seriousness. "Makes a man feel good to be held in such respect."

"I'm so sorry," said Karolina, but Alex was well aware that she was still laughing. "Was that your reaction to my saying I could kiss you? I have never had that happen before! It's quite flattering actually!"

"No of course not!" said Alex, although just for a second, he couldn't stop the thought passing through his mind of what it would be like to be kissed by Karolina. "No, I just mis-stepped and fell into those baskets. They really shouldn't allow them to be stacked all over the pavement like that. People are bound to be falling over them all the time!"

"I'm sure you're right, Alex. All the same, in the interests of your safety, I hereby withdraw my offer to kiss you."

Alex had no idea whether that made him feel better or worse and he certainly didn't know what to say in response, but he was saved from having to come up with a quick witty response by Karolina.

"Getting back to your idea, we get an old jewellery box and use it as bait. We pretend it is full of Constantine's jewels, to draw the murderer out?"

"Yes, that's pretty much it." Alex felt a little put out that he hadn't had the pleasure of detailing his plan to her, because she'd come up with the same idea, so fast.

"I think that's great! Let's get going and find some suitable bait!" So saying, she turned and began to walk down the narrow street, looking purposefully into each shop as she passed. Alex gathered himself together and walked as quickly as he could to catch up with her.

They continued to explore more streets, being greeted by the shopkeepers with cheerful calls of "Kaliméra". They stopped frequently to admire the various items they were offered for sale. At a stall selling walking sticks and wooden cooking utensils, they found and bought a jewellery box made from olive wood that would be perfect for their plan. The top had a carved image of two dolphins arranged nose to tail to form a circle. Karolina explained that as well as the jewellery box they also needed to buy several other parcels to act as camouflage for the bait, should they be seen by the murderer when they arrived back at the hotel. Alex expressed some doubt about how necessary the subterfuge of the extra packages was, but Karolina enthusiastically insisted it was essential and bought several items from different vendors as they explored the streets. Alex ended up carrying several parcels wrapped in old newspapers and tied up with string. Alex was carrying the parcels awkwardly, with his stick in one hand and with the parcels tucked under his other arm. Karolina had pointed out that she was also capable of carrying some, if not all of the packages, but Alex had stubbornly refused to give them up.

Eventually they found themselves back in the small square with the café again. Stamatis came out of the taverna and greeted them with a cheerful "Kaliméra!" as if greeting old friends. He offered them the same table as the day before, but reluctantly they declined and made to continue past the taverna. Stamatis, seeing Alex struggling with his parcels turned and ran back into the taverna. He came out almost immediately with a small boy of about ten years old. Refusing to take any notice of Alex's polite refusal, Stamatis took the parcels from Alex and gave them to the boy, before waving the trio on their way. Now with the small boy happily following along carrying their parcels they continued to wander through the streets. No more than another fifty yards further on, the three of them emerged from the narrow streets onto the quay of the old harbour. The small boy carrying the parcels had attached himself to Karolina and seemed to be fascinated by her blonde hair, looking up at her constantly. His English was good and he and Karolina were soon chatting away. Alex looked around him at the harbour and at the several colourfully painted fishing boats that were tied up at the quay. Their owners were busily gutting and cleaning their catches on the quay and selling them wherever they could to passers-by.

After a few minutes enjoying the sites of the harbour, they decided to leave and follow a different route back to the hotel. They followed a path through the narrow alleyways that lay underneath the walls of the huge fortress that protected the port.

"Venetian?" suggested Alex, looking up at the fortress.

"Definitely," agreed Karolina.

"Thought so," said Alex and nodded knowledgably, in happy agreement.

By mid-morning, they were back at the hotel.

Chapter 22

The driver had returned from town with the repaired radiator earlier that morning and by now was hard at work refitting it. Shortly before lunchtime he had finished to his satisfaction and the travellers began to make preparations to depart. While two men from the hotel collected baggage from the rooms and loaded them onto the omnibus, the driver and passengers sat down for a simple light luncheon provided by the hotel. Alex noted that Sir Alfred chose to sit with Mrs. Webster, while Mr. Webster, Dai and Vasiliki sat at another table. Mr. Webster and Dai were in deep conversation again. Lord Thomas appeared to have luncheoned earlier and was not to be seen. Soon the driver began walking around the passenger's tables, waving his arms vigorously, as if he were herding a flock of chickens. The weather this afternoon was much hotter than yesterday. Reluctantly the passengers finished their meals and drinks and began moving slowly towards the old converted military truck. Lord Thomas emerged from the hotel and joined the line waiting to board the omnibus. Several passengers decided the process was progressing too slowly so they sat back down at the benches in front of the hotel to wait for those around the truck to sort themselves out. Eventually, all was loaded. The driver cranked the engine which seemed as slow to get going as the passengers had been. Once the engine started the driver ground the omnibus into gear and moved off. If the passengers had forgotten why they had felt reluctant to board the vehicle, they were very quickly reminded. Once on the move they were bumped and jolted as the vehicle rolled slowly ever eastward along the rough road. Karolina thought that the padding on the simple bench seats seemed even thinner today than yesterday.

As they left the more populated area around Rethymno, the omnibus once again became a thing of joy to children, who raced the slow-moving vehicle until their legs got too tired or they ran to the side of the road to wave up at the passengers. Most of the road running East lay close to the sea, providing them again with wonderful views of the Mediterranean. Farmers and field workers stopped their work for a moment and waved at the passengers on the colourfully painted omnibus. Sheep and goats in the fields also interrupted their grazing to stare at the omnibus as it passed by. The scent of pine trees and the occasional eucalyptus tree seemed particularly strong in the warmth of the afternoon sun. The road ran past small villages nestling at the seas edge and alongside enticing sandy beaches.

After a couple of hours of driving, they pulled over at a small roadside taverna for drinks and a chance to stretch their legs. The sea was only yards away. It looked cool and inviting. The waves gently rolled in and out, covering and uncovering the fine yellow sand.

Alex waited for a quiet moment and when Karolina was separated from the rest of the passengers went to stand next to her, looking out over the beach to the sea. "I've indulged myself in a little bribery," said Alex, quietly.

Karolina looked up at him with interest.

"I've given the driver a nice little tip and made sure that when we get to Knossos, he'll pull up outside the address for Constantine's granddaughter, Ariadne. I got it off that letter we found in his attaché case."

"Good thinking."

"When we arrive and while we're all milling around outside, can you try to get in to talk to Ariadne privately and explain our trap? Then bring her out and I can make a show of presenting her with our condolences and Constantine's luggage, including the fake jewellery box. I'll make sure everyone sees it. I've already locked the box and I'll keep the key, so she doesn't need to open it. Just look at it, then put it aside. While I'm doing all that, can you keep your eyes . . . " when Alex mentioned her eyes, he made the mistake of looking into Karolina's eyes and saw she was looking at him intently. He momentarily forgot what he was saying, " . . . eyes, you know, keep your eyes . . . open? That's the thing – keep your eyes open and see if any of our suspects react."

"Got it," said Karolina.

"Good. Very good. Well, I suppose we'd best get back on the old boneshaker then?"

"You don't think we've got a chance to go for a swim first?" asked Karolina innocently.

"What? No. I shouldn't think so. Have you got a bathing suit? Sorry. Rude of me to have asked that. Too personal. Sorry." Alex ran his finger round his shirt collar and decided it was really much hotter this afternoon.

Karolina smiled up at him. "Just teasing you Alex," and walked off still smiling over her shoulder at him.

"Damn!" said Alex to himself. "Damn. Damn. Damn! Every time. Every damn time."

Murder on Crete

As it had earlier in the journey, conversation petered out as the omnibus worked its way slowly along the road to Knossos. The passengers continued to be bumped and shaken about as before, but to her surprise Karolina felt herself starting to drift off to sleep. She blamed it on the heat of the afternoon and possibly on the cold glass of white wine at the last rest stop. Now, she thought longingly of that cold drink, with condensation forming and dripping down the outside of the glass.

Suddenly she shook herself awake! This wouldn't do at all. She decided that in order to stay awake she would go over everything she knew about the murder. Alex had come up with a great idea, using the fake jewellery box to catch the murderer. Maybe she could solve it before the trap was even sprung! It wasn't that she was being competitive, she told herself. It was that she wanted to show Alex that she could come up with good ideas too! She could pull her own weight! She was determined she wouldn't be a Watson to Alex's Sherlock! That was better! Now she was wide awake again.

She loved reading. What was it those detectives in novels were always going on about? Means, motive and opportunity. Good. Now she was focused. Sure, Alex wasn't as stupid as she had first thought. He was quite intelligent really, but he was so naïve! He was just a boy! Suddenly she leant forward and tapped him on his shoulder. He turned round and looked at her questioningly.

"How old are you?"

"Er. . . Twenty-Five."

"Good." She sat back in her seat, then waved her hand at him to show she was finished.

After a second or two he turned back to the front with a puzzled expression on his face.

Lord Thomas who was seated next to him looked at the passing scenery with an amused smile on his face.

So Alex was actually older than she was, but surely she was more mature. She'd seen and experienced so much more of life than he had. She caught herself. She had forgotten about the battles he had been in. The things he would have seen. The things that had happened to him onboard that ship, where was it? Jackland? She didn't even know where that was. She didn't know what family he had left after his father had died. She didn't know if he worked for a living or was of 'independent means' as the English liked to describe it.

She leant forward and poked him hard in the shoulder. He jumped, then turned round again and looked at her questioningly again.

"What's your job?"

"I work for the Admiralty."

"Doing what?"

He suddenly looked very uncomfortable. "Er . . . just paperwork shuffling. That sort of thing you know."

That didn't mean anything to her. She would work on that later. She sat back in her seat and waved her hand at him again to show he could turn back to the front again.

Lord Thomas was enjoying eavesdropping on their conversation and found Alex's discomfort quietly amusing. He turned to Alex. "Out of interest old man, what is it exactly that you do for the Admiralty?"

"Not really supposed to talk about it Lord Thomas. A bit hush-hush. You know how it is?"

Murder on Crete

Lord Thomas nodded. Some of his friends spoke of similar things. Lord Thomas wondered if maybe he'd been underestimating the young man. He knew better than to ask for more details. It just wasn't done. But maybe when he got back to London, he'd mention Alex's name around his club and see if there was any response.

Meanwhile Karolina was also struggling with realising that she knew so little about Alex, but she'd told him a lot about herself and her parents. She'd told him how she felt about Randolph for God's sake! She was only now realising that he had avoided saying more than the odd word or two about his own background. Had he done that deliberately? She clenched her jaw. She wasn't going to let him get away with that! He'd said he'd grow up on a small farm, hadn't he? Farmers boy, quite attractive, but not too bright she'd thought at the time. But hadn't he said he'd gone to college? Studied to be an accountant or some such, but failed his exams? Damn! She hadn't paid any attention! She looked at the back of his head, sat in front of her. He was very naïve. But in a quite attractive way she thought. Some girls would probably actually describe him as handsome. Damn! What was she doing? Now he was distracting her from solving the murder! Concentrate Karolina. Concentrate. What would Sherlock and Watson do? 'Means, Motive and Opportunity'. That was it!

Who were the suspects? After the alarm had been raised, Lord Thomas had been waiting for them on the promenade deck, so he had opportunity. He would also have had the means to toss the much smaller Doctor Constantine overboard. Although in her eyes he was quite old, he still looked fit. Perhaps not as well muscled as Alex. Alex did have a good body, but his bad leg distracted you, and at first you didn't notice his other qualities. He carried himself well.

He had a proud upright stance, probably from the navy. He also had a nice smile. 'Stop it!' she berated herself, 'get back to Lord Thomas and the murder'. Lord Thomas had means and opportunity but what about motive? There was the medical scandal, but Alex had said he didn't think he had known about Doctor Constantine's past until Alex had shown Tommy the business card. She just couldn't see Tommy as a cold-blooded murderer but maybe he could lose his temper in a fit of rage? She didn't know. Who else had opportunity? Mr. Webster? Was he on the promenade? His wife had said they were both in their stateroom, but that was on the promenade deck. She could be giving him a false alibi. He could easily have tipped Doctor Constantine over the side and got back to the stateroom before he was seen. She didn't know for sure that Doctor Constantine had been responsible for their daughter's death, but it fitted together like a jigsaw. But he was such a quiet man and she'd watched his reaction when they discussed Doctor Constantine's death. She was sure he had shown genuine concern over the granddaughter. But as Alex had said, maybe that was guilt? Who was a more likely suspect? Sir Alfred! Was that because she just didn't like the man? He was the epitome of the selfish entitled aristocratic Englishman. She cringed when she thought of the ingratiating, unctuous approaches he had made to her. She also had seen his temper snap several times. Yes, he could have done it in a fit of anger, that was means. He had the motive as well. She was sure he was short of money. If Sir Alfred was desperate enough to be selling family heirlooms, then he was desperate enough to have tried to get his money back that he'd lost playing cards with the doctor. Means and motive and he had also been on the promenade deck at the right time. Means, motive and opportunity . . . and the clincher was she didn't like him!

In the interest of impartiality, she also felt she couldn't yet eliminate the other suspect who also had opportunity – Dai Williams. Although initially he came across as a friendly jovial Welshman, she believed he had a much darker side that sometimes appeared. That was when his affable nature and his accent disappeared. There was a harder, tougher man under the seemingly simple, happy exterior. She imagined that he could well be nasty enough to kill if he had a strong enough motive. Money, or valuable artefacts would provide him with that motive. Yes, Mr Dafyyd Williams need to stay on her suspect list.

Her head nodding with the motion of the old truck, her eyes started to droop. Without realising it she drifted off. A picture of Alex, wearing a deerstalker hat and smoking a pipe, following her into her dreams.

Chapter 23

A little while later, they came out of the hills and wound down a steep road. Suddenly they could see the Temple of Knossos laid out in front of them. The temple ruins covered a low hill in the middle of a valley. On one side of the valley a Greek orthodox church together with a few small houses looked across to the temple on it's central hill. On the other side of the valley a larger village and a Catholic monastery looked out across the valley at the temple atop it's hill.

The first to see Knossos was Mrs. Webster, who gasped and without taking her eyes of it, shook her husband awake so he too could see it. Their excited exclamations woke those of the other passengers who had drifted off to sleep. Soon they were all craning around each other to get a better look. The driver, hearing the exclamations and conversation that started up around him, pulled the truck to a stop in the middle of the road.

The driver and passengers all disembarked and walked forward from the truck to get a better view.

The ruins spread out below them, covered several acres of the valley. Pointing to them he said "Knossos". Then, making imaginary bull's horns on his forehead with his fingers, he lowered his head and swung it around looking at his passengers.

"Minotaur!" said Karolina.

"Yes!" said the driver "You speak good Greek. What that is in English?"

"Minotaur," said Karolina and they both laughed.

Murder on Crete

"Tommy come look! That large open space in the middle is the central court. To the right, the tallest structure is the hall of the colonnades. That's where the archaeologists are working at the moment. I can't wait to join them!"

"It's much larger than I expected," said Lord Thomas looking at the extent of the ruins. The hill was almost completely covered by a complex maze of newly excavated wall foundations. "How old do you think it is?"

Karolina saw that an audience had gathered around her. "It's bronze age. It was first built in about 2,000 BC, but we think it was rebuilt after a huge earthquake a few hundred years later. We haven't fully finished excavating the entire site, but we think it will cover three or four acres."

"Who lived there, dear?" asked Mrs. Webster.

"The king of the Minoans – King Minos. The story goes that he was the son of Europa and Zeus. King Minos asked Poseidon, the god of the oceans and of earthquakes for a gift. He promised that he would sacrifice the gift back to the gods. Poseidon sent Minos a beautiful white bull but it was so beautiful that King Minos decided not to sacrifice it but to keep it. That made Poseidon angry so to teach him a lesson he made King Minos's wife fall in love with the bull. Pretty soon she bore a child. It had the body of a boy but the head of a bull. This was the Minotaur. The boy's appearance exposed his wife's unfaithfulness and King Minos was not at all happy, so he had a labyrinth constructed - take a look at the maze of walls down there! - and banished the Minotaur to the labyrinth. To keep the Minotaur in the maze, every few years, seven girls and seven boys had to be sent in to the maze to be killed by the Minotaur. And so it went on, until one year Theseus, Poseidon's son, volunteered be one of the sacrifices. Being either sneaky, or clever, or both, he first seduced King Minos's daughter Ariadne, who gave him a ball of string as a reward. Not much of a gift if you ask me, so maybe he wasn't such a great lover! Anyway, after tying one end of the string to the entrance of the maze Theseus entered the maze, tracked down the Minotaur and killed him. In some stories he killed him with his bare hands. Then using the string, he found his way out of the maze."

"Oh dear," said Mrs. Webster, "Some of these Greek myths are quite awful, aren't they?"

"Oh, I don't think so Mrs. Webster," replied Karolina, "I think they're absolutely wonderful! I also find it interesting that in the myth, King Minos made the god Poseidon angry and Poseidon was the god of the seas and of earthquakes. Now, science seems to have discovered that King Minos's palace at Knossos was destroyed by an earthquake. There's a lesson to all of us there. Be careful which gods you offend!"

Sir Alfred and Dai had walked away while Karolina was telling the story, but the rest had gathered around her.

"Do you really think that's a labyrinth down there?" asked Lord Thomas. I give you it looks like it was a huge palace with lots of rooms and corridors. And it is bewilderingly complicated and would be easy to get lost in it, but is that the same as a labyrinth?"

"Well, they say everything has to originate from somewhere, even myths. But a couple of interesting things about the origins of the word labyrinth. The word is linked to the Minoan word 'labrys' or 'double axe', which is the symbol of the Minoan mother goddess of Crete. You're sure to see examples of that if you wander around the palace. Also, as you go around you may see carvings of another symbol in various places. It looks really like a simplified square or circular drawing of your Hampton Court maze. That symbol is also often associated with Crete, and Knossos. So there really does seem like Knossos could be the origin of the myth of the labyrinth."

The driver began to do his chicken herding mime again so the passengers began to make their way back to the omnibus. Once everyone was aboard the driver began cranking over the engine. After several minutes, with no result, both the passengers and the driver were beginning to run short on patience. The driver was obviously also beginning to run short on energy to crank.

Straightening his back and breathing deeply he took a break. When he'd recovered rather than resume cranking, he opened the left-hand engine panel and folded it back along the centre of the bonnet. Taking a handful of tools from the running board toolbox his head and shoulders disappeared under the bonnet. Metal on metal noises accompanied by mute cursing emerged. After five or ten minutes he straightened up and moved to the front of the truck. Grasping the crank in his right hand he paused, then, with great determination he swung hard. He was rewarded with an explosive bang that caused a stifle scream from Mrs. Webster. It was followed quickly by two other rapid explosions before, grumbling, the engine started and began idling with an uneven rhythm. Smiling proudly in triumph the driver quickly folded down the engine compartment panel, slamming it shut, then jumped up into the driving seat and ground the truck into gear. Slowly they started the descent towards the village.

Alex twisted and leant back over his seat to talk to Karolina. "So you remember what to do when we get there?" he said.

"Yes I do. Do you think I'm an idiot?"

"Yes, of course," said Alex, "I mean, yes of course you remember and no of course you're not an idiot. Sorry. Shouldn't have said anything," and he turned back to watch the road in front of him. Karolina thought she may have heard him muttering something like "Damn" under his breath.

Chapter 24

It only took a few minutes to cover the half mile or so to the village and for the driver to pull up in front of the address he had been given, but Alex was seriously worried that the truck might not even get that far. It moved even slower than before and its progress was marked by repeated backfires. When the driver eventually brought it to a halt and stopped the engine, he jumped straight out and opened the engine cover again.

The passengers climbed down and stretched their arms and legs and strolled around the truck looking at the village.

They were parked in a small square, with a white stone fountain in the middle. Leading out of the square ahead of them the main street was lined by small shops and tavernas. Dominating the square itself was what appeared to be a Christian abbey or monastery. It loomed over the village, three or four stories high, with high arched windows. In the centre was a tall square tower. Smaller, less grandiose buildings lined the square stretching out from the monastery. The building they had pulled up in front of looked like this building had once been part of the monastery. Possibly a refectory or some such. Three low steps led up to a heavy oak double door framed on either side by nine-foot columns and surmounted by a broad classical Greek pediment. Underneath the pediment was a small carving of the Madonna and child.

Karolina moved unobtrusively towards the door as Alex went and stood beside the truck. "How long before you can get this old thing going?" he asked, in a voice that carried across the square. This had the desired effect of drawing attention towards him and the driver and away from Karolina. The driver straightened up and shrugged, whether from his lack of mechanical knowledge or from his lack of English it was hard to tell. Karolina, looked around at her fellow passengers and choosing her moment, tried the door to the refectory. Finding it unlocked, she slipped in.

Closing the door behind her, she called out to announce her arrival to whoever was around. Soon, a very pretty young girl of about eighteen years old with long straight, black hair tied back in a pony tail came in to the entrance hall and greeted Karolina in Greek.

"Oh. Good afternoon. Would you be Ariadne?"

She switched effortlessly to English, "Yes miss, I am."

"I'm so glad to meet you. We've just arrived from Chania and we have your grandfathers' luggage with us. I'm so very sorry about you grandfather."

Ariadne's face fell at the mention of her grandfather. "Thank you miss," replied Ariadne quietly, then took a breath and composed herself. "I received a telegram informing me of your intended arrival. Thank you so much for helping in this way. It's very kind of you."

"Your English is extremely good," said Karolina and was pleased to see the bright smile return to the young girl's face.

"Thank you miss. I have plenty of practice. I run this house to provide boarding for the archaeologists working on the temple. Most of them are English or American and I enjoy talking to them in the evening. Shall I come outside and get my grandfather's things?"

"Oh yes. Please do, but before we go outside, can I share something with you?"

Murder on Crete

The girl stopped and tilted her head to the side, waiting for Karolina to continue.

Sitting on the truck, watching the scenery unfold on the way to Knossos, Karolina had been thinking about what she would say when this moment came. She had decided that telling the young girl that her grandfather had been murdered would be un-necessarily distressing for her at this time. That should wait until their suspicions were either confirmed or disproved and they could tell her more certainly exactly what had happened. She had decided to only reveal their suspicions about the attempted robbery. "Someone has searched you grandfather's luggage several times on the way here. We think that whoever that was has been trying to steal something of great value from your grandfather's luggage. I don't suppose you have any idea what that object might be?"

Ariadne silently shook her head, fully absorbed in what Karolina was saying.

"Well, to try and smoke out . . . " realising that such a colloquialism might confuse the girl, Karolina re-phrased her statement, ". . . sorry. I mean that in order to trap the thief we have added some bait to the luggage. We have added a small jewellery box that we hope the thief will think it was part of your grandfathers' luggage."

"So when the thief sees it . . . "

" . . . he will give himself away. Exactly!"

Ariadne nodded decisively, "So what would you like me to do?"

"Nothing really, when my friend hands over the luggage and the empty jewellery box, just act normal, unconcerned and we will watch for any giveaway reactions."

"I understand," said Ariadne.

"Great. By the way, please forgive me. I should have introduced myself. My name is Karolina McAllister."

Karolina offered Ariadne her hand and she reached out and grasped it. Suddenly the young girl looked close to tears and Karolina pulled her in to hug her.

Once they had both regained their composure, Karolina led Ariadne outside onto the steps.

Alex, together with most of the passengers, were gathered around the front of the truck, where the driver was the centre of attention as he worked on the truck's engine. Alex looked up as Ariadne emerged from the refectory and then turned and tapped the driver on the shoulder. The driver stopped working on the engine and wiped his dirty hands down the front of his old trousers. Alex had obviously explained to him what would happen and the driver walked round to the back of the truck, grabbed Constantine's trunk with one hand and picked up the suitcase with his other. Dragging the trunk and carrying the suitcase, he approached Ariadne and dropped them both at her side. Alex picked up Constantine's attaché case and put it under his arm that held his stick, then, taking the jewel box from his own bag, he walked across and stood in front of Ariadne.

"Miss Ariadne, please accept our most heartfelt sympathy for the loss of your grandfather. Although we that met him did not know him well, we know he spoke so very fondly of you and was very happy to think that he would be seeing you again soon. Although that isn't to be, please accept the condolences of all of us, together with those of Captain Meunier," and Alex handed her the jewellery box.

Murder on Crete

Alex thought that he'd made a good attempt to express their sympathy and condolences to the young girl and had also made sure everyone had a chance to see him hand over the jewellery box. He was taken by surprise and horribly embarrassed therefore when she burst into tears, threw her arms round his neck and sobbed onto his shoulder. Frozen in place he had no idea what to do, how to politely extricate himself from the situation. He felt a blush rising in his cheeks.

Karolina watched him standing there with the young and very attractive girl hanging from his neck, pressed against his chest. She almost forgot that she was supposed to be watching the reactions in the other passengers. Mrs Webster, was dabbing her eyes with a handkerchief. Mr. Webster and Lord Thomas were watching the scene with concern in their eye, while Dai stood with his head bowed. Sir Alfred seemed unconcerned and distracted and was glancing over his shoulder at the truck. Vasiliki however, was a revelation! When Alex had first appeared with the jewellery box, shock and surprise passed across his face, to be replaced in seconds, by what Karolina could only describe as a vicious snarl. A second or two later, he had wiped off all expression from his face but stood frozen to the spot, watching intently as Alex had presented the box to Ariadne.

Vasiliki was still staring fixedly at the jewellery box and was oblivious to the fact that he had been observed. The last thing she wanted was for him to realise he was being watched so she turned away and for the moment paid her attention to Alex being embraced by Ariadne.

Meanwhile, Mrs. Webster had come forward to where Ariadne and Alex were standing. She gently disengaged Ariadne from Alex and then put her own arms around her. Mr. Webster joined his wife and also put his arms around both of their shoulders. After a few moments, Mrs. Webster took out her handkerchief and dabbed Ariadne's eyes dry. Ariadne eventually pulled away and asked all the passengers to come in to the refectory for refreshments and so that she could thank them properly.

The entrance hall inside the refectory was large and square. The walls were of undressed stone, with a sturdy fireplace of a finer stone on the wall opposite the double door. The fireplace had a high mantlepiece. Each of the fireplace uprights had been carved with angels. Standing either side of the fireplace were two tall, heavy-looking, dark wood armoires. Either side of the door back out to the square were coatracks, hung with waterproofs, coats and large hats. Two smaller doors led out of the room into other areas of the building. A mismatched collection of dark wooden chairs was scattered around the room, together with a number of small three-legged tables. The walls were hung with dark oil paintings, mostly featuring religious scenes. The driver followed Ariadne into the room carrying the trunk with Dai behind carrying the rest of Constantine's luggage. Ariadne walked across to the fireplace and placed the jewellery box on the mantlepiece. Two elderly Greek women dressed in long heavy dark skirts, elbow-length white blouses, red and black patterned waistcoats and headscarves had entered by the internal door on the right. Ariadne spoke to them briefly, before they left to organise refreshments.

Murder on Crete

As the passengers gathered, Alex sidled over to Karolina and without looking at her said quietly so no one else could hear, "Did it work? Did you see any reaction?"

"Oh boy did it work! It was exactly as you planned. As soon as you produced the bait and handed it over to Ariadne, he just couldn't hide his surprise and anger!"

"Whose surprise?"

"Vasiliki!"

"But it couldn't have been him! He wasn't even on the promenade deck when Constantine was murdered."

"But it could," contradicted Karolina, who had had a few seconds longer to think about it. "Why are you thinking that Constantine was thrown from the promenade deck? You said the scene didn't make sense to you. I think Vasiliki killed the doctor in his cabin. Then he staged the scene using the bloody pillow case to smear blood and positioning the pipe and spectacles by the handrail. Then, back down to Constantine's cabin where he'd left the body. Quickly tip him over the rail, then create a perfect alibi for himself, by pointing up to the promenade deck and saying that was where the body fell from!"

Alex looked at her. It did fit together. "If you're right and I think you are, we have a bigger problem. I was talking to the driver before you came out with Ariadne. He has given up on getting the truck working again today. He thinks we're going to have to stay here tonight. We've just passed the bait to Ariadne and put her in real danger!"

They both looked across the room towards Ariadne, who was talking to the driver. He was firmly shaking his head as she asked him questions. She stopped and thought for a few seconds, then coming to her decision, raised her voice and addressed the passengers. "Sirs and Ladies," she called out. "Your driver tells me that your vehicle will not be able to proceed further tonight. However, here in this building we provide accommodation for the archaeologists and students who do the work on the excavation of the Temple of Knossos. At the moment, there are no workers staying here, so we have plenty of rooms. I apologise that they are basic and surely not as luxurious as you are used to, but I am pleased to offer them and for you to be my guests this evening."

Many of the passengers made noises of appreciation, the most obvious exception being Sir Alfred, who immediately turned to Lord Thomas and began to complain loudly. Mr. and Mrs. Webster made their way over to Ariadne to continue to offer her their support. Out of the corner of their eyes, Alex and Karolina carefully watched Vasiliki and saw an expression of cold calculation on his face as he looked towards the fireplace, with the jewellery box still sitting on the mantlepiece.

Chapter 25

Heavy drapes covered the two windows from the entrance hall to the street, letting in only the slightest glimmer of moonlight. Being the middle of the night, the hall was silent and dark.

A very acute listener might have just made out a small creak that came from the floorboards outside the door that led from the sleeping rooms. A louder click, as the handle of the door was turned was more noticeable. There was a pause of a few seconds before the door slowly began to swing open into the room. Someone with eyes accustomed to the low light, might have been able to make out the dark shape of a man slowly and stealthily crossing from the door to the fireplace. Something made a scrapping sound as it was dragged quietly off the mantlepiece.

"I really don't think that's yours to take, you know," Alex's calm voice rang out and he stepped out from behind the armoire next to the fireplace. The flashlight in his hand came to light. In its beam stood Vasiliki. The jewellery box was in his hands and an angry snarl was on his face.

"You think you can stop me taking it if I want too? A cripple who can barely walk?" He sneered.

"You could probably take it if you really wanted to, but all that's inside it is a few stones from the roadside."

"Then where are the jewels he was carrying?" snarled Vasiliki

"How do you know he was carrying jewels?"

"The stupid old man would talk too much when he got drunk. I would overhear him boasting to his friends in the cassino. That was when I decided to follow him to Crete. He said he was taking an heirloom of great value to his granddaughter. I thought it would be easy to take it from an old man like him. Where have you hidden the jewels?"

"I'm afraid you're going to be disappointed old chap. There were no jewels."

"I don't believe you!" You're no better than that old man! He wouldn't tell me where they were either. He caught me searching his luggage. I tried to beat it out of him, but he fell and died before I could make him tell me. But I'll make sure you tell me first, before I kill you."

Vasiliki held the jewellery box close to his body in his left hand, but he extended his right hand in front of him. The light from Alex's flashlight glinted on a silvery steel blade.

"That's a mistake, Vasiliki," said Alex quietly, not looking down at the knife but concentrating on Vasiliki's eyes, looking for any forewarning of an attack.

Suddenly Alex's stick came up in a backhand curve and smashed down on Vasiliki's extended wrist with a loud crack. Vasiliki howled in pain and dropped the knife. He flung a huge roundhouse punch at Alex's face, but Alex threw up his forearm still holding his stick in his hand and blocked it. Without pausing, he took Vasiliki by surprise with a powerful jab to the front of his face. Frustrated and even more angry, with blood pouring down his face, Vasiliki advanced on Alex and threw another roundhouse punch. Alex blocked it again, but enough of Vasiliki's momentum was transferred to Alex's arm that he had to step back to maintain his balance. That was disastrous for Alex. As his weight transferred to his bad leg, the leg failed to lock and collapsed beneath him. He fell backward away from Vasiliki onto the floor.

Vasiliki stood above him. He raised the jewellery box in both hands above his head, ready to smash it down into Alex's face.

A quite metallic click behind his head stopped him.

"That's the sound of a single action Smith and Wesson 38, being cocked," said Karolina, calmly. Even though she spoke quietly, her voice was filled with unmistakeable threat.

"You may think that a woman might be too scared to pull the trigger, but you would be wrong."

As he realised his goal was going to be permanently denied to him, Vasiliki could not control the rage building in him any longer. A roar slowly grew in his throat, as he swung round with the jewellery box high, to smash it down on Karolina.

A loud explosion filled the room.

Chapter 26

Next morning, Karolina was surprised that she had managed to get any sleep at all in the night, but although her head was filled with swirling thoughts to begin with, she had fallen asleep quite quickly. Of course, she'd had no sleep at all while she had been hiding in amongst the coats and waterproofs by the door, waiting for Vasiliki to make his play. The huge adrenalin surge when he did appear had brought her wide awake throughout the confrontation and had been slow to disappear afterwards. Once it was all over, she had retired to her basic, bare little room and fallen asleep in the cot bed. Waking up very early this morning she knew she would be unable to go back to sleep, so she had decided to stay with her usual routine of being one of the first to rise.

Coming into the breakfast room she saw that she had only been beaten down to breakfast by Dafyyd Williams. On seeing her enter, Dai had risen solemnly from his chair, made a slow deep bow, then smiling touched his hand to his imaginary cap, saluting her with a smile. He then left the breakfast room to return to his room leaving her in peace, without saying a word.

Silently flattered, Karolina made her way through to the breakfast room and through it to the patio outside. She selected a table in the early morning sun and settled herself down to read her book before breakfast.

It was sometime later when she was joined by Alex, who politely stood by the other chair and asked if he could join her.

She nodded and gestured to the vacant chair.

"I have to say, thank you again for last night," said Alex

"You're welcome, of course."

"Where on earth did you get that Smith and Wesson! I had no idea you were carrying it!"

"It was a birthday present . . . from my mother. A girl feels a little more comfortable when she has something like that to back her up."

"I image you would," said Alex. "All the same, a little bit of luck helps as well."

"I'm sorry?"

"Well, catching him in the thigh like that. Put him straight down on the floor! Lucky shot!"

Slowly Alex realised that Karolina had not responding to him, but was silently staring him hard in the eyes.

"You think it was a lucky shot," she said quietly, but with the volume building

Belatedly, Alex realised his mistake. He shut his mouth firmly and said nothing.

"A lucky shot!" and her voice continued to rise. "I'll have you know I could shoot the head off a rattlesnake at fifty feet when I was twelve years old! Even in the dark, I could have hit any part of Vasiliki I wanted! I aimed for his leg! I damn well aimed for his leg! I knew I didn't need to kill him! I damn well aimed for his damn leg!"

Karolina sat in her chair fuming at Alex.

"Sorry," he said quietly.

She still sat there, glaring at him. "And another thing! What about you yesterday? Grabbing poor Ariadne like that!"

"What?"

"I saw you! We all saw you! Standing there with that young girl in your arms, holding her to your big manly chest! Smiling like a Cheshire cat. Don't deny that you were enjoying it. You should be ashamed of yourself!"

"Sorry." He said again, even more quietly.

"I should damn well think so!" said Karolina and lapsed into fuming silence.

At that moment, Ariadne came out onto the patio and giving them both a big smile, asked what they would like for breakfast. Karolina, smiled sweetly at her and ordered toast, a selection of pastries, fruit, coffee and orange juice. Alex just said, "Coffee," without making eye contact with Ariadne.

After she left, Karolina said, "There's no need to be rude to her!"

"Sorry."

"Stop saying sorry!"

"Sor. . . "

"Look. Let's start again. Good morning. How are you? I hope you slept well. Thank you, I slept well too. Do you know how the man I shot last night is?"

Nervously Alex said, "Someone told me the police officers had taken him to the hospital which is only a mile or so away, further down the valley."

"Someone told you? You mean Ariadne told you?"

"Might have been." Alex admitted a little nervously.

"Good. He was bleeding pretty badly. Hope they got the bullet out and stitched him up in time."

"The police told some . . . they told Ariadne . . . that just about everyone heard him confessing as he ranted and raved, lying on the floor, so they think there will be no trouble when he stands trial."

"Oh yes! He said some pretty nasty things about you and me too. I was quite flattered actually!"

"Do you enjoy getting under people's skin?"

"What do you mean by that?"

"Sorry. I mean . . . Oh damn it Karolina! . . ."

Karolina actually broke out into a smile. "Do I get under your skin too Alex?" she said sweetly.

"You know you do. You always get me tangled up and saying the wrong sort of stuff, 'cos I can't think straight!"

"Well, I'm sorry too Alex," she said still smiling. "I really don't plan to annoy you, but sometimes it's simply too tempting to resist. But I'll try not to do it so much. Except of course when I can't resist it," and she treated Alex to an even bigger smile.

By now, Ariadne had arrived with breakfast for Karolina and coffee for Alex and this time Alex made a point of nervously saying thank you to her.

They both began to eat their breakfast and enjoy the view from the patio, which looked out across the valley where ruined walls and olive trees could be seen. Already, farmers were at work, taking care of the olive trees.

"I've been reading this book I borrowed from Doctor Constantine," said Karolina, pointing to the book lying closed on the table. You've probably not heard of something called 'Linear A and Linear B' before?"

Absently, sipping his coffee and looking out at the view across the valley and lost in his own thoughts, Alex mumbled, "Linear writing. An as yet undeciphered ancient writing system, probably Greek. Linear as in straight lines cut into clay tablets, as opposed to cuneiform that uses wedge shaped depressions made by pushing a stylus into the clay." Looking as if he had suddenly woken up, he jerked upright and looked at Karolina.

Her mouth dropped open and she stared at him.

"What . . . on . . . earth."

"Sorry. Linear A and Linear B. Ancient writing systems," Alex said apologetically.

"How do you know that? she demanded. "What did you say you studied at college?"

"Er. . . Mathematics." He said worriedly.

"Then, how on earth do you know so much about Linear A and Linear B?"

"Well, chap I work with," babbled Alex. "Awfully nice chap. Name of Dilly, actually his name is Dillwyn, but we all call him Dilly. Bit of a professor I suppose, Cambridge, I think. He reads ancient languages, so we talk about that a bit. No one can read it you see. Linear A and B, I mean. Undeciphered. Got a bath in his office actually . . ." Like a car running out of fuel, Alex slowly ran out of things to say.

Karolina was not going to let his strange outburst rest at that, but she refused to let herself be distracted, so, for the moment she pushed it to the back of her mind, to bring it back up again at a better time.

"Anyway, since you're such an expert on Linear A and Linear B," she said and she looked carefully at Alex to see his reaction. "Since you're a know-it-all, I wondered what you thought this was." She opened Constantine's book and thumbed through the pages to find one that she had previously marked with a bookmark. She showed the page to Alex. It showed a picture of several pieces of brown or orange clay tablets covered in tiny symbols mostly consisting of combinations of straight lines in different orientations.

Karolina explained, "Crete has given us an awful lot of pieces of clay tablets marked like this."

Alex looked at the picture. "Linear A and Linear B tablets" he said, puzzled, looking up at Karolina.

"Not the picture. Look at the handwritten notes around the edge."

Around the edge of the picture ran twenty or thirty handwritten symbols, also consisting of similar, but different arrangements of straight lines.

Karolina said, "At first I thought someone was comparing another inscription, or maybe trying to write an example of Linear A or B . . . ?"

A slow, wide smile grew across Alex's face and he looked from the book to Karolina.

"You know that even though we have found Constantine's murderer and he's confessed to the murder, we still haven't solved all of the mystery."

Karolina looked at Alex with a puzzled expression on her face.

"We've heard several people say that Constantine was bragging about bringing something of great value to his granddaughter.'

"But we found nothing when we searched his luggage, not even in his trunk," objected Karolina.

"That was because there was nothing there. He had given that object to someone else to carry."

"Who?"

"You!"

Karolina quickly looked down at the open book and the handwritten notes around the edge of the page. "You know what this is, don't you?"

"Yes. It's an ancient code system called Rosicrucian that goes back at least to the 17th century."

"Can you read it?"

"If it's just the basic, single level encryption and not using several different layers of encryption then yes, I should be able to decrypt it."

"How does it work?"

"Well, first you draw four frames, two like noughts and crosses, two like large 'X's."

"What's 'noughts and crosses' mean?" asked Karolina.

"Sorry. I think you call it tic-tac-toe' don't you?"

Karolina nodded.

"So, the tic-tac-toe frames have nine spaces each and the 'X' frames have four spaces each – top, bottom, up, down. That's 9 + 9 + 4 + 4 = 26, so you write the 26 letters of the alphabet, in alphabetic sequence, in those spaces. So 'A' goes in the top left corner of the first tic-tac-toe frame."

Karolina nodded. She was following the explanation closely.

"So, the top left corner of the tic-tac-toe frame, is made up of a bottom horizontal line, joined to a vertical line on its right, right? So, the code for 'A' translates as that combination of lines. The final thing is that to distinguish between the two tic-tac-toe frames, the second frame includes a dot in its symbols. Same for the two 'X' frames, the second frame has a dot in its symbols."

Alex saw Ariadne at the far end of the patio and called her over. "Ariadne, could I please have a pencil and some blank sheets of paper?" Ariadne nodded and returned a minute or two later with the requested items. Alex said to her, "You might like to remain if you have the time. This may be something important for you." Ariadne looked puzzled but obediently came closer and looked at the open book on the table.

Alex quickly took the note pad and drew the four frames he had described and filled in the spaces in the frame, with the twenty-six letters of the alphabet, in alphabetic sequence.

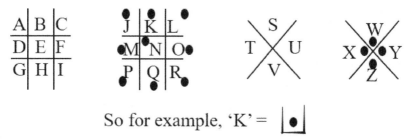

So for example, 'K' =

He paused then and looked up. "This may be good enough if this is the only level of encryption but it is possible the message uses a second level of encryption. The letters may not simply be positioned using a simple alphabetic sequence. That would make it more difficult, but not impossible, to decode"

"Okay, just get on with it and we'll soon know if this is going to work," said Karolina.

Alex copied out the handwritten symbols from the book. They fell into six groups.

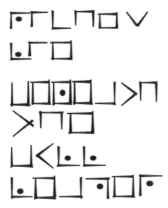

Alex explained, "The first symbol has a horizontal and a vertical line, so it belongs to one of the tic-tac-toe grids and since it also has the spot, it tells us it's in the second tic-tac-toe grid. The only space in the grid with two lines that match that symbol is the bottom right corner. So, we decrypt it as 'R'."

"Then the next character is 'I, then 'C' and 'H', followed by . . . 'E' and finally 'S'."

"R-I-C-H-E-S!" said Karolina excitedly. "Come on. Why have you stopped?"

Moving to the second block of characters, Alex wrote 'L-I-E'.

"Riches Lie . . . , Don't Stop! It's working!"

Alex moved on to the next block of characters . . .

As he wrote, he read out loud, "Riches Lie Beneath The . . "

Then he wrote 'B-U-L-L'.

He stopped and looked from Karolina to Ariadne. Karolina growled at Alex, "If you stop one more time, I'm taking that jug of water and pouring it over your head!"

Alex laughed and decrypted the final block of characters, before reading them back.

"L-E-A-P-E-R. Riches Lie Beneath The Bull Leaper. What on earth is a bull leaper?" said Alex.

Karolina replied, "All over Crete you find frescos, mosaics, carvings of bull leapers. They were a key symbol in Minoan culture. They all show athletes, typically boys and girls, around bulls. The bulls are charging the athletes. At the last second the athlete grasps both of the bull's horns and does a cartwheel over the head of the bull and lands behind the bull."

"We have a carving here," said Ariadne, pointing behind her to the centre of the patio. Alex and Karolina leaped up from the table and followed Ariadne to the centre of the patio. Sure enough, a circular stone was engraved with a picture of a charging bull and an athlete grasping the horns with both hands, ready to leap over the bull's head.

Ariadne left them staring at the carving and ran to get a crowbar. She and was back with it in less than a minute.

Alex took the crowbar and pushed the edge in the gap between the carved stone and the patio bricks. Levering upwards, the stone resisted, then suddenly sprang upwards. Karolina grabbed the edge and tipped the stone backwards. Taking the crowbar from Alex she scraped in the dirt that had been exposed.

"There's something here!" She dug deeper and then levered a strong heavy metal box from the soil. Kneeling on the patio, she prised the lid from the box.

Wrapped in multiple layers of oil cloth was a carved wooden box, ironically very similar to the bait jewellery box that they had purchased in Rethymno.

Karolina straightened up and looked at Ariadne. "You should open this. It's from your grandfather."

Reverently, Ariadne took the box from her. Slowly she removed the lid. Sunlight glinted off gold, lying on black velvet in the box. Karolina and Ariadne both gasped as they saw the beautiful pair of intricately wrought, large gold earrings lying in the box. They were each made from a gold hoop, about four inches in diameter, each hoop in the form of a two headed snake. From each hoop hung eight small coin-like golden discs and eight tiny gold owls. Inside the hoop connected by four delicate gold chains was larger disc. Engraved upon this gold centrepiece was an image of a bull's head with a graceful female athlete cartwheeling between its horns. "They're so beautiful!" said Karolina.

Holding the box safely in one hand, Ariadne threw her arms around Karolina and hugged long and hard. Tears ran down both their cheeks. Releasing Karolina, she did the same to Alex. Alex awkwardly held his arms straight out behind Ariadne, without touching her, looking worriedly towards Karolina.

After a few seconds, Karolina growled, "All right. Enough. . . Enough!"

Without understanding what had gone on, Ariadne let go of Alex and turned looking between the two of them, excited and happy beyond words.

Epilogue

Alex sat on the patio, legs stretched out, ankles crossed in front of him, a cool glass of white wine on the table beside him and a book in hand.

He'd dropped the book into his lap and was just sitting there, idly watching the countryside in front of him, feeling relaxed and comfortable.

He'd been down to the dig again this morning, but after lunch decided to rest up at the refectory. Although he enjoyed his repeated visits to the dig site, after a while not being able to get down on his hands and knees and do his bit became a little frustrating.

Ariadne approached his table with the bottle of white wine and a questioning look on her face but he smiled and shook his head. She nodded and went back inside.

Ariadne had not been able to thank Alex and Karolina enough after the finding of the treasure. She had shown the earrings to Arthur Evans. He was sure that they were Minoan earrings, made in Crete around 1600 B.C. He had offered to show them to the Heraklion Archaeological Museum to see if they would purchase them and had reassured her that she was likely to receive a very attractive offer from them. Ariadne had told both Alex and Karolina that they were welcome to stay with her for as long as they wished. Karolina especially had become good friends with the young girl.

Alex thought that Karolina seemed to be really enjoying being physically active, working on the dig. It was also keeping her fully occupied mentally and after a few attempts to discover how Alex knew so much about undeciphered scripts and ancient secret codes, she'd seemed to forget about it. Apparently, she just put it down to Alex's idiosyncratic Englishness. He'd not been forced to reveal anything about his work for the secret 'Room 40' department of British Admiralty, not that that he had been asked to be part of the new Government Code & Cypher School that was in the process of being formed.

Alex had telegrammed Charlie to let him know he would be staying on a few more days in Knossos so that he could take advantage of this time to explore the temple. He had no way of knowing that when Charlie had read his telegram a slow smile had spread across his face and to his wife's surprise he had reached out and squeezed her hand, before kissing her affectionately. Charlie suspected he would be hearing more of Alex Armstrong and Karolina McAllister's adventures, in the very near future.

Notes About This Book

The research for a book like this is tremendously enjoyable. Much more important than mere historical or geographical accuracy is uncovering stories that you were unaware of. Finding all those lost pieces of history that you don't quite believe even when they come from trusted sources. Checking when something was invented or something happened. One slight anachronism I have to own up to is 'sunglasses'. Today they are inseparable from enjoying the sun, but although Foster Grant was founded in 1919, their sunglasses didn't really become popular until later in the 1920's. However, details aside the stories that come to light are delightful.

Take for instance Mrs. Edith Stoney. She did present a lecture on the Physics and Mathematics of Steam Turbine Engines at King's College for Women. Edith and her sister Florence did also setup and operate the new X-ray services in several field hospitals during the Great War (the one to end all wars!). She did win the French Croix de Guerre medal for her work. Today, a similar achievement would be remarkable. To do all that in the years before 1918, when no women were allowed to vote in parliamentary elections, simply incredible! It is a small honour for me to be able to publicise her achievement in this story.

It is also true that the French government did run a competition to develop a drink for French soldiers that would make quinine more palatable and the winner was Dubonnet (only the French!)

Murder on Crete

The British Royal Navy has some interesting traditions. As is mentioned and many people are aware, they are responsible for the term 'Limey' as applied to anyone British. The navy also salutes differently to the other armed forces. Rather than showing the palm of the hand, they turn their palm downward. This was to hide their palms which were typically stained and dirty from working with tarred rigging. As Captain Meunier also correctly points out they make toasts while seated. Why? Visit H.M.S. Victory and note the head room in the cabins!

In the trenches, the healthier American soldiers did seem to suffer more from influenza than the poorly rationed English tommy.

However, the story is not a full and accurate description of the battle of Jutland. It was much more terrible than outlined in this novel. Alex's story is similar to one real life account, but others were much more traumatic and many of course did not survive to tell their tales. If you are interested, look up the story of Jack Cornwell, a delivery boy who enlisted in the navy at fifteen without his father's permission. As 'Boy Seaman First-Class' he was killed at the battle of Jutland at sixteen and was then awarded the Victoria Cross, posthumously, for his bravery. The loss of many British ships at Jutland did occur, including three battleships with more than a thousand men on each. Some say that in order to maintain the high rate of fire for which the Royal Navy was justifiably proud, shortcuts were taken. To get the ammunition quicky enough from the magazines to the guns, bulk head doors were left open. When German shells struck in just the right place the battleships magazines exploded literally blowing the battleships to pieces.

Murder on Crete

Watching the destruction, Vice Admiral Sir David Beatty is quoted as making what may be one of the greatest understatements of all time, "There seems to be something wrong with our bloody ships today." Indeed there was. Over 6,000 British sailors died at Jutland. The epitaph on Boy Seaman First-Class Jack Cornwell's grave reads, 'It is not wealth or ancestry but honourable conduct and a noble disposition that maketh men great'. Sir Alfred, please take note!

Another person that I'm pleased to honour in this story, is Alex's colleague "Dilly". Dilly Knox was one of the key members of the British Admiralty cryptography team called 'Room 40' and later GC&CS, who made such valuable contributions and saved so many British lives, during WW1. He continued to work in cryptography including participating in the cracking of the Enigma machine until he died in WW2. Also significant in my view is his unique achievement of getting a bath installed in his office in the Admiralty, in which he would repose while at work on various cryptological puzzles.

If Ariadne's treasure interests you then the original idea for the earrings can currently be seen in the Cretan Section of the British Museum.

One final piece of research, that I am determined to personally verify next time I'm in Crete is the origin of the dish called 'Imam Bayildi' or 'Help, the imam has fallen.' Any food with a story that amusing about it just has to be delicious!

Murder on Crete

Thank you for reading this story. If you like it, then please leave a review on Amazon. If you would like to hear more from Alex and Karolina, then please follow me, M.C Juan-Stanley. If you didn't like it, well then my name is Sir Arthur Conan Doyle.

Printed in Great Britain
by Amazon